The Royal Diaries

Marie Antoinette

Princess of Versailles

BY KATHRYN LASKY

Scholastic Inc. New York

Vienna, Austria 1769

January 1, 1769
Hofburg Palace, Vienna, Austria

I do solemnly promise to write in this diary given to me by my tutor, Abbé de Vermond, if not every day, at least every week, even though writing is not easy for me. For I shape my letters poorly and do not too often know the proper spelling. Still, this is my resolution for the new year.

    Yours truly,
Archduchess Maria Antonia Josepha Johanna, daughter of Maria Theresa of Habsburg, Empress of the Holy Roman Empire of the Germanic Nations, and the late Emperor Francis of Lorraine

January 3, 1769

My second time writing. I am keeping the resolution. Abbé de Vermond would be proud. I spelled the word *solemnly* correctly, too, I think. I am grateful to the Abbé for giving me this beautiful little diary. It is blue, the color of the sky, and has gold *fleurs de lis* engraved — the symbol of the French Court — or one of the many symbols. I must learn all the symbols of the French Court. I must learn French! Here now I shall list all the things I must learn over the next year:

- to write and read French (I speak it well, as it is the language of the Court here)
- gambling
- to dance in the French manner
- to walk, in the manner of the French Court, as if I float in the immense panniers, or side hoops, of the French ladies' dresses
- to read better
- to write better

Why must I learn these things better than other girls my age, better than any of my sisters or brothers, of which I have fifteen? Why? Because I am to be Queen of France. More about that later. My hand and my brain are too tired to explain.

January 4, 1769

I now am refreshed so I shall explain. I am just thirteen and before I become Queen, I must first be what the French call the *Dauphine.* It is their word for the highest Princess in the land. The Dauphine is the wife of the Dauphin, the eldest son of the King. The French King is Louis XV. His son died. So now his eldest grandson is the Dauphin. His name is Louis Auguste. I am to marry him, probably next year. And when Louis XV dies, the Dauphin shall become King Louis XVI and I shall become Queen Marie Antoinette. Together we shall rule. But for now I am an Archduchess. I am thirteen and everyone calls me Antonia. I am not yet ready to be a Dauphine, let alone a Queen. Everyone tells me this at least sixteen times a day.

Here is a list of the people who tell me this:

·Mama, the Empress
·Countess Lerchenfeld, my Grand Mistress,
    or governess. I call her Lulu for short.

·Noverre, my dance instructor
·Monsieur Larseneur, the French hairdresser
·Abbé de Vermond, the French tutor
·many brothers and sisters

I am not ready because I do not write or read in my own language well, not to mention French. Although I am a better reader than a writer, I just hate to read. But I am not stupid. I think some thought I was stupid. But Abbé de Vermond told Mama that I am "clever" and that I am "capable of learning and eager to please" but that I am a bit lazy. He gave me this diary because he thought that if I had someplace private to put my innermost thoughts, I would be more eager to write and thus improve my awful handwriting and spelling. He promises never to read it and, best of all, never to tell Mama I am keeping it. That is important because Mama is very nosy. Extremely nosy. I spelled that word, *extremely*, right. The Abbé would be very pleased but he shall never see it, if he keeps his promise. And I shall keep mine to him to keep writing. It does become easier each day. I think soon I shall write some more about my innermost thoughts. I'll make a list of the topics now for next time so I won't forget.

·Nosy Mama
·Caroline, my dearest sister
·My fat dead awful sister-in-law
·My favorite niece

January 5, 1769

This is fun. And Abbé de Vermond says I am improving in my writing and my reading. Already! And it has been only five days.

Now to my list.

1) Nosy Mama — I love the Empress my mother very much. But she and I are quite different. She is not so lazy as me. She never wastes a minute. Indeed, when she was in labor giving birth to me she called a dentist to come along with the midwife, for she decided to have an old rotten tooth pulled at the same time. She felt it was efficient to be in pain all at one time for two things. She is very orderly. Nothing is ever out of place. I misplace my handkerchief all the time and I lost my fan, the good one, that belonged to Brandy, my old governess whom Lulu replaced. Mama never forgets or misplaces things. But Mama is nosy. She wants to know everything I am doing, every bit I am

learning. She tries to peek when I am getting dressed or undressed. She worries that my bosom might remain too flat, but with Caroline I remember her worrying that her bosom might be too large. "A heavy bosom adds age to a young girl." That is one of Mama's sayings. She has many sayings, including the family motto, which she recites all the time. "Others make war, but thou, oh happy Austria, make marriages." These words are written in Latin on many crests and emblems around the palace. But that is not enough for Mama. She says it all the time — in Latin, in French, in German, and in Italian.

Mama's goal is to marry all of us children off to Kings or Queens, Princes or Princesses, Dukes or Duchesses. That is how the Empire grows, gets new land, and friends or allies to help us in times of war. Through marriage we can perhaps get peace. It is a very good bargain, in Mama's mind.

I think that is why Mama is so nosy. To make marriages, she must stick her nose into all of our businesses. So far she has done well. My sister Maria Christina married Albert of Saxony, and he is now governor of the Austrian Netherlands, the part we call Hungary. Maria Amalia married the Duke of Parma and is therefore a

Duchess in Italy. My brother Joseph married fat Josepha of Bavaria, and my favorite sister Caroline was wed to Ferdinand, King of Naples.

Mama would be more nosy with us children if she had time, but because she is the Empress she is always working. Sometimes we go two weeks without seeing Mama. If someone were to ask me my very first memory of Mama, I would say it was when Brandy led me into her rooms of state at the summer palace, Schönbrunn, and Mama looked up from her papers. She had been peering at them through a large magnifying glass and she continued to hold it up and began to peer at me.

I had not intended to write this much. I am tired. My hand needs a rest. I shall find my brother Ferdinand and play shuttlecocks.

January 9, 1769

I am continuing my list concerning my innermost thoughts. Number two is Caroline. Do I say *is* or *was*? She is not dead but she is not here, either. It has been almost a year since I have seen her. Mama insisted that she marry Ferdinand of Naples. You see, my sister Josepha, who was older than Caroline, was supposed to marry him but Josepha died — the smallpox. So Mama insisted that Caroline "step in," as she put it. I loved Caroline dearly. She is three years older but we were very close. We were as close as . . . let me think . . . bees and honey or roses and thorns.

chicks in a nest
leaves to a twig
bark to a tree trunk

You might think me nasty for saying this, but Caroline would be the first to agree. You see, I am considered quite pretty with my blue eyes and ash blonde hair and very fair skin. Caroline is not. She is rather stumpy and very ruddy of face, prickly on the outside but lovely and beautiful inside. No matter, every rose must have its thorns — Caroline herself once explained this to me. And Caroline provided the thorns. She is fierce and independent, and she always protected me just as the thorns protect the rose from greedy people in a garden. She made an uproar when Mama insisted she marry the King of Naples. Mama said such an outburst was thoughtless and rude. But I loved Caroline with all my heart. She writes me, but it is not the same Caroline. She seems sad and almost weak in her letters.

I love my sister Elizabeth, too, but poor Elizabeth hardly comes out of her apartments. You see, Elizabeth was once a great beauty, really much more beautiful than I am, and very charming and witty, but she was stricken with smallpox. Her skin is deeply pitted. Elizabeth is twelve years older than I and she had been promised as a bride to the Duke of Bavaria, but of course it could not be, once her skin was ruined. She stays in her rooms now, heavily veiled, but at Schönbrunn in the summer she feels freer and wears thinner veils.

Before Caroline left for her marriage, I had really learned as much from her as from any of my governesses and maybe even more than from Abbé de Vermond.

Now number three on my list: Josepha, my sister-in-law. No one liked Josepha, not even my brother who was married to her. Mama made him marry her. Josepha was miserable, cranky, ugly, selfish, and whiney. She caught the smallpox and died. No one was too sad. But Mama felt we had to pretend. She said we must appear to grieve. It was only proper. So she insisted that my older sister, who was by coincidence also named Josepha, visit her tomb.

Well, the body was still warm in the coffin and the terrible pox must still have been alive in the air, because the very next day our dear sister came down ill and was dead within three days.

Josepha had been promised to Ferdinand of Naples as his wife. So that is when Mama insisted that Caroline take her place. So I lost two dear sisters just because of that miserable Josepha's death and, yes, Mama's notions about what is proper and a duty. God forgive me for these words but if I cannot help but think them, is it that much worse to write them down in this diary? And remember, God, I am writing this diary so that I might become a more learned person and fulfill Mama's wishes that I become Queen of France.

Enough! It makes me sad, and now the snow comes down thickly and we have been promised a sledge ride.

January 11, 1769

Today we went sledge riding and sledding. My dear little niece Theresa, or Titi as I call her, comes with us now that she is over her cold. She is just seven. She and I rode on the same sled. She rides stretched out on my back and we go whizzing down the slope. There are better slopes at Schönbrunn Palace out in the country. Here in Vienna there are not that many. It is too flat. But if we can get permission from the chief of the Imperial Guard, then Hans is allowed to take us across the river Danube to the other side where the Vienna woods slope down to the river. We then go to the Hermannskögel, which is the highest point in Vienna. We hope to go there tomorrow.

January 13, 1769

No time to write. Fresh snow and we have permission to go to the Hermannskögel. Titi and I are so excited!

January 14, 1769

No more sledge riding or sledding. Mama was furious when we returned the last time. First I was late for my music lesson with Master Gluck. Mama came in to scold me for being late, as I had just begun on my scales. Mama takes our music education very seriously. She says we live in the center of the best music in the entire world. For everyone knows that Vienna is where all the greatest musicians live and study and work. She even goes as far as to say that the music gets worse as soon as one leaves the city proper and keeps getting worse the farther one is from Vienna. She hates to think of what the music will be like in France, and in England, she cannot imagine.

In any case, when she came into the room, she lifted my hands from the harp. They were red from the cold, and she said, "Daughter! These are not the hands of an Archduchess, nor shall they ever be the hands of the Queen of France at this rate. You look like a scullery maid!"

She then ordered me to sleep in chicken-skin gloves. I hate more than anything those chicken-skin gloves. Even Lulu looked pained by the suggestion. It is an awful feeling, not to mention the odor of sleeping with chicken skin. But it is true that they whiten and soften the hands. Mama was so worried about Caroline's ruddy complexion that she had specially made for her a chicken-skin mask for sleeping that fitted over her eyes and cheeks. But Caroline took it off the moment she got in bed and the governesses weren't looking, and then the next day she would just powder her face more heavily. I wish I had Caroline's nerve in standing up to Mama sometimes. Except did it give Caroline what she wanted? She still had to marry that ugly old fellow from Naples.

January 19, 1769

Very boring days with no sledge driving. Monsieur Larseneur came today to work with my hair. They say that my forehead is too high and that my hairline is too far back. This is because Brandy, my old governess, used to always pull my hair back so tightly when I went to bed. It caused it to thin and break. Monsieur Larseneur is a fashionable Parisian *friseur*, as they call hairdressers in France. He does many of the Ladies-in-Waiting at the Court of Versailles. He is very friendly and we have nice chats. I learn how to spell many French words about hair from him. Here I'll make a list:

cheveux = hair
peigner = to comb one's hair
se coiffer = to do one's hair

se friser = to curl one's hair
épingle à cheveux = hairpin

You see, I am learning French. But I am bored. *J'ai beaucoup d'ennui.* That is French for "I have much boredom." I want to be sledge driving with my dog Schnitzel or my darling Titi.

January 20, 1769

Oh, I am so bored with the hair and the lessons and the dancing. But Lulu says they must get me near perfect very soon, for a French painter is to make my portrait and then a miniature that will be sent to King Louis and the Dauphin. Mama feels if they see how pretty I really am it shall speed the official engagement. You see, although this has all been planned since I was nine years old, it is not yet official, no date has been set, and that all depends on the French King. I wonder what the Dauphin looks like. Maybe they are trying to get him ready for a portrait. He is probably terribly handsome, as his grandfather the King is said to be the handsomest reigning monarch in Europe. I have heard that King Frederick the Great of Prussia is quite handsome but one dare not even whisper that name in front of Mama. Frederick is her great enemy. It is because of Frederick that we must all marry so well. Almost twenty years ago, just after Mama became Empress, Frederick invaded Silesia, part of our hereditary lands and our richest province. Mama never got over losing Silesia and vowed she would not sacrifice another centimeter to The Monster, as she calls King Frederick. She still vows to recover Silesia and we, her daughters and sons, are part of her plan. We lay siege not through weapons of destruction but through marriages.

So I must learn to dance. My hairline must grow back. I must improve my reading and writing and card playing. Card playing and gambling are favorite pastimes of the French Court of Versailles. All this is not so easy. I suppose marching and being shot at is harder, but not so boring.

January 23, 1769

Imagine this: while I practice walking with a book on my head to balance in the most immense panniers I have ever seen, which they tell me are quite the mode at Versailles, Abbé de Vermond reads aloud to me the history of France.

This of course was Mama's idea. "She can listen while she walks. She has ears as well as feet." Thank you, Mama. There is a special walk for the ladies of Versailles that has to be mastered. One must take very small, quick steps. This makes one's dress float over the polished marble floors.

January 30, 1769

Lulu tells me that Mama is very worried because King Louis has not yet sent a formal letter concerning my marriage. He apparently was supposed to do so by the end of this month. I always get worried when Mama gets worried, because she makes us, whichever child is worrying her the most, go with her to Papa's tomb at the church of the Capuchins to pray.

February 1, 1769

Guess where I was today — the Capuchins church with Mama. Oh, I just hate it. I was nine years old when Papa died, and Mama has rarely worn anything but black since then. She cut her hair and she painted her apartments black. Now her hair has grown and her apartments are painted gray. But still the coffin she ordered made for herself at the time of Papa's death sits in the burial vault of the chapel beside Papa's, waiting for her. So Mama goes every afternoon and sits there beside the two coffins, the one with Papa's bones, the other empty, and prays. And today she brought me, too, to pray for my marriage, to pray for Silesia, to pray for good fortune against The Monster.

February 4, 1769

I do not think I shall ever learn to dance as well as Lulu. Today in my dance lesson, not ballet but ballroom, Master Noverre asked Lulu to dance with him to show me one of the special Court dances. Lulu is so graceful. She appears to almost float. Lulu has reddish hair and when she dances her cheeks flush and her gray eyes grow all sparkly. I could tell Noverre was completely taken with her, and the violinist, who until then had just been scratching out his tunes for my awkward feet, suddenly played with new life.

P.S. Forgot to mention that Mama received a letter from the French Court saying a dentist will be coming to examine my teeth. Mama takes this as a very good sign. It means they are still interested in me.

She also beamed today when Abbé de Vermond told her of my remarkable progress in reading and writing.

February 5, 1769

We go to the Opera tonight at the Burgtheater. Although I do love the Opera, I am nervous because one time when we went, nearly two years ago, the most embarrassing thing happened and I have never forgotten. I blush still when I think of it. Mama had not come with us, but Josepha and Caroline and Ferdinand and I were all sitting in the Imperial box when suddenly Mama rushed in, and right in the middle of the performance during the soprano's aria, Mama cried out to the audience, "My Leopold has a son!" Our brother Leopold is the Grand Duke of Tuscany. His first son, Francis, named for our father, had been born, and Mama was so excited with this first grandson that she had to interrupt the performance. I nearly crawled under the seat. I turned as red as the velvet cushions in our box. I still cannot think of it without cringing. I doubt if there was ever a girl in the Empire so embarrassed by her mother. But at least tonight there are no babies expected.

February 6, 1769

The Opera was wonderful, although Lulu felt that the tenor might have had a cold. Lulu has a very good ear for these things. There was, however, one discomforting thing about going to the Opera this year — no, no birth announcements, but I was made to sit in the front row of the Imperial box. Usually this is reserved for the Empress and my eldest brother, Joseph, and his wife, though of course now she is dead. But this time I was made to sit there and I could feel the stares of the people. I was on display and Mama had given me to wear her own diamond necklace with the star sapphire pendant, and they had corseted me to within a centimeter of my life. I could scarcely breathe through the first act until my stays loosened themselves. I know why this is now. Lulu explained. They want to show me to the people as the future Queen of France, but also there was a large French delegation there, in particular the

Duc de Choiseul, the French ambassador, and our own Prince Kaunitz, our most important diplomat, was by his side. He and Choiseul were the two men who drafted the Versailles Treaty in 1756, and they are the ones who thought up the idea of my marrying the Dauphin, I think even before Mama thought of it. That, knowing Mama, seems almost impossible. Well, anyhow, they are the ones who must make the marriage contract and tend to all the details. So that was why I was on display.

February 8, 1769

If I thought I was on display at the Opera it was nothing compared to the ball tonight. I had to spend four hours with Monsieur Larseneur. He insisted on doing my hair in the latest Court style. You might wonder how all this took four hours. Well, here is what they did to my hair. They first divided much of it into skinny little bunches and then twisted them tightly and pinned them to my head so it looked as if at least a hundred snails had crawled up and settled on my skull. Then they pinned pads of horsehair atop those snails. To these pads they attached false braids. Then they caked with pomatum, a kind of spicy-smelling ointment, the rest of my own hair that was loose, sprinkled on powder, and finally they piled it up very high. So high you would not believe it. Into this structure Monsieur Larseneur twined silk roses and toy birds with real feathers. I tucked one away in my pocket to give to Titi, for I knew she would love it. All that took four hours.

The dress I wore was beautiful, made of a violet blue satin with the French lace sleeve ruffles called *engageantes* that quiver with your every movement. But this was the strangest of all. Beneath all the flounces, and attached to the whalebones of the hoops, were half a dozen or more small glass vials the shape of teardrops with stoppers in them, and in the bottom of each vial was a drop of honey. Even Mama was confused when she saw them attaching these to my hoops. "What is this?" she asked.

"Ah, Madame Empress," the French seamstress said. "This is for the fleas."

"What?" exclaimed Mama. "My daughter is not a dog. She has not fleas."

"Ah, non! Non, Madame Empress. 'Tis not your daughter

who draws the fleas. It is the pomade in her hair and the wheat flour paste that draws them."

"Seems impractical," Mama sniffed and walked away.

But impractical or not, if this is what it takes to make a marriage with a man who will be the King of France, then, why, of course!

February 9, 1769

I'll tell you what impractical is ———— having to sleep with one's head on a wooden block. Yes, that is what I had to do in order to preserve this hairdo that took four hours to build. I had to preserve it because there is yet another ball tonight and I am on display again. So my hair shall be perfect but my eyes will be red.

February 10, 1769

The best thing about the ball last night was watching Lulu dance. And then for the last dance Master Noverre and Lulu did the Scottish reel. Everyone loved it. Mama insisted they do it again.

February 11, 1769

Today in my dance lesson I complimented Master Noverre on his dancing last night and said I hoped that by the time I was married to the Dauphin, I could do the Scottish reel well enough to teach my future husband. Master Noverre's face creased with great concern. "No! No, Your Highness. The Scottish reel is not permitted at the Court of Versailles." I was astounded and asked whyever not. He just said they had their rules, their etiquette, and it would be considered too savage for the court. I never heard of such a silly thing in all my life. The dance is fun and lively. Some of those stupid Court dances are so slow and boring, I nearly fall asleep on my feet doing them.

February 12, 1769

I think that my days of privacy are numbered. I have many odd thoughts about this marriage. It is hard to explain. It is not that I don't want it. I want to meet, and I am sure that I shall love, the Dauphin, but there is so much more. The Court of Versailles I think is quite different from our Imperial Court in Vienna. Versailles is a very complicated place. They have many complicated games. That is why I must learn gambling. But that is not all. Lulu says that they have special ways of doing everything. Only certain people can pour the Royal Family's wine at the dining table, and getting dressed is also very complicated. Here I just have Liesel or Brunhilda to help me into my petticoats, and sometimes Lulu oversees the lacing of the corset, but in France at the Court of Versailles, it is not a simple chambermaid who ever touches the Dauphine's or the Queen's undergarments. No, it is the *Femme d'Honneur,* or Lady of Honor — a highborn lady only is allowed to help with petticoats and camisoles and the "body linen." Yes, that is what they call it there. Caroline and I call such garments "underprivates." We made up the word ourselves. Well, Caroline did. She is so clever with things like that.

Now Lulu tells me only the Lady of Honor helps with the body linen, but it is the tirewoman, a kind of chambermaid, who carries away the soiled linens after the Queen or Dauphine has worn them. And to assist the tirewoman there is an undertirewoman who does something else, and it is a grave error to ask the wrong person to take the wrong garment at the wrong time. How shall I ever learn all this? Lulu says she will make me a chart showing who does what. But how can I commit such a chart to memory right now when I also have to learn that stupid pluperfect tense in French that I don't even think we have in German, or if we do I have never heard of it. This is all too much!

February 14, 1769

The balls were fine and Mama was most pleased with the impression I made. And last night was the first night that I could sleep with my head on a pillow and not on a block. It took Lulu and Liesel forever to scrub the pomatum and powder from my hair. Did I mention that I wore the Ruby of India diamond necklace? They had wanted to tint the hair powder pink, for they thought it would set off the ruby better, but I disagreed. I said blue was the only color, pale blue to go with my dress, and then the red of the ruby would really stand out. Mama complimented me on this decision and also my improving French. Still, Mama's French is so much better. Sometimes I think it would be easiest if Mama married King Louis XV, seeing that she is already an Empress and he is King. I suppose there would be a problem as to which country and palace they would live in. But Mama is so skillful with all these things. She loves speaking French and in particular she loves calling King Frederick of Prussia a monster in French. You should see how she pronounces and accents the word when she is speaking to the Duc de Choiseul or others from the French Court. "Le Monnnnnnstre!" and she drags out the word so that her face drops into a perfect oval shape and her eyes nearly pop out.

February 18, 1769

I mentioned to Lulu, in jest, or so I thought, my idea of Mama marrying King Louis XV, and Lulu gave me a very dark look. I said, "What's wrong? He's a widower. Mama is a widow. Why not?" And she looked even darker and crimped her mouth shut. "Tell me!" I demanded.

So she said that the King has a very close woman friend, a mistress named du Barry, Madame du Barry, and it is building to a scandal, for she might be coming to Court.

So I said "Oh," very quietly. Then Lulu added, "She is quite coarse. Very common."

Well, that is terrible, I thought. Then Lulu muttered "from the streets." I nearly gasped. No, not nearly. I did gasp.

Now I am really confused. How can there be a Court where a royal person has "street friends" and yet at the same time in this Court there are countless rules of etiquette about who can pour the King's wine and who can hand a Queen her chemise? I think I shall be completely lost when I get there.

February 27, 1769

I know it has been a whole week since I have written, but I have been most upset. For almost a year now, ever since Caroline went away to marry the King of Naples, I have wondered why she has sent so few letters and they seemed to be in a voice that I did not recognize as Caroline's. Well, now I know. The answer was right under my own nose the whole time. In my closet is a trunk with my old dolls and their clothes. I had not played with them for a while, but when Titi was in my apartments today, I thought what fun to bring them out so we could dress them and perhaps even pomade and powder their hair in the latest Parisian fashions. Caroline and I used to spend hours playing with the dolls in the trunk, and she must have known that sooner or later I would look there. And what did I find tucked under the chemise of our favorite doll but a letter, not in Caroline's hand but in Mama's to Caroline. And here is what it says, for I will copy it into this diary. It was written on August 19, 1767, right after Mama told Caroline that she was to marry Ferdinand of Naples, right after Caroline went screaming through the halls and I went running to Mama to beg her to send Ferdinand away.

> *Dear Caroline:*
>
> *It is time for you to grow up. I shall not tolerate fits and scenes from your little sister Antonia about this marriage. I warn you now that you will be totally separated from your sister Antonia, for I see that she is constantly discouraging you from the marriage and telling you all sorts of bad things about Ferdinand. It does not matter if a man is fat*

or thin, handsome or ugly. He will make you a good husband. He has territory and brings strength to our Empire against the monster Frederick. Little Antonia does a disservice to you, to me, and to the Empire by her unruly behavior. I therefore forbid any secret contact with her. You shall be watched carefully, so dare not violate my command by seeking solace or communication with your silly little sister. You must do your duty to me and the Empire and you shall do it by marrying Ferdinand, King of Naples. Remember, it is more important to become a Queen than remain a sister and a spinster.

Sincerely, your mother, Maria Theresa, Empress of the Holy Roman Empire

So there it is. That is why Caroline's letters, which hardly ever come, sound so unlike her when they do come! Both of us, Caroline in Naples and I here in Vienna, are spied on constantly. I am so angry with Mama for this, I hope I do not have to see her for at least a week. I do not know how I could ever hide my anger. I realize that there is probably no one I can trust. Not even Lulu, for Lulu's life depends on pleasing Mama. Of course, Titi did not know what was wrong with me and I couldn't exactly tell her. So I had to hold back my tears and go on playing dolls with her as if nothing had happened.

Titi found some little tiny bauble in the bottom of the trunk and fashioned a necklace from it for the doll she was playing with. She then powdered her hair and tinted it blue. "Look, Auntie. It's you. The most beautiful lady in the Empire. It's you, the Queen of France. *C'est magnifique!*" Titi exclaimed and I laughed gaily at her French and said how clever she was, and then suddenly in the midst of my laughter, I had this odd thought and tears spilled out. Titi kept asking what was wrong and I kept saying, "Nothing, nothing at all." But my thought was, of course I must be magnificent, for when one is either on display or being spied upon it will not do to look dingy. I must sparkle. I must always sparkle whether I laugh or cry. I must dazzle and then no one will see the real me. I shall just be this bright and shining thing. Oh, Diary, I am so thankful that I have you. But now I think that I must start hiding you, even though you have a key, for yes, there are spies all around.

March 4, 1769

Nearly a week without seeing Mama. She has been in constant meetings with the Duc de Choiseul and the other French ambassador, the Marquis Durfort. Every day I don't see Mama is good, for it gives me more strength for the time when I will see her. I am still very angry but I think I can hide it better. And if there is one thing I do not want to do, it is to cry in front of Mama.

Even though I don't see Mama, there are messages and notes from her every day. One came just this morning telling me that she has instructed Abbé de Vermond in his French history lessons with me to familiarize me with the names of all the French colonels and the colors of their regiments. This is very much like Mama. They say that in 1756, when The Monster marched into Saxony and war broke out once again between our Empire and the Prussians, Mama personally checked many of the supplies being sent to the soldiers at the front line. She insisted that one lot of blankets be exchanged for another, for they were too thin to keep the dear brave soldiers warm, and she even pawned many of her jewels in order to better equip the soldiers at the front.

March 5, 1769

Another message from Mama today instructing me that I should devote even more time to the study of the reign of Louis XIV, who ruled France in the early part of this century and of whom I am a descendant.

March 6, 1769

Oh dear, Mama wants to see me today. I am so nervous. I know she is going to quiz me on Louis XIV and the colors of the regiments.

March 7, 1769

No quiz at all. Mama was in the best of moods. A portrait painter has been sent from France to paint me with the intention of taking back my likeness to King Louis and the Dauphin. Mama is beside herself. She was practically dancing around Kaunitz, tweaking his beard, her eyes glittering. "We are coming closer, closer, Mein Prince," she kept saying. "And you, my little *bijou* (*bijou* means jewel in French), we must have Larseneur work on your hair.

The hairline is coming back. Look, Kaunitz." And she brought me over to the prince and had him examine my forehead. "And how is the dancing going with Noverre?" she asked next.

"Mama, I am to be still in the portrait and not dancing or even walking," I said. And everyone laughed very heartily, Mama the heartiest of all. Then she pinched my cheek and called me her little *Leibenkügel,* which means "sweet cake," and do you know, this is the only time I ever remember Mama using such tenderness with me. Then she said, "You see, Gentlemen," for not only was Kaunitz there but Mama's ambassador to Versailles, Count Mercy d'Argenteau, as well. "You see, Gentlemen," she said, "she has wit, this one. She will be a match for any of those women in the Court of Versailles." But there was something in the way Mama said "those women" that made a chill run through me. It was as if she did not respect them or felt they were bad in some way, and if this be true, why is Mama sending me there? I wanted to ask her but I was frightened.

March 10, 1769

The French painter arrived today. His name is Monsieur Ducreux and he is a specialist with pastels. He actually has been instructed to paint not only my portrait but others in my family as well. When Mama heard this, her eyes narrowed, but then she said in German, so I trust Ducreux did not understand, that she knew what the French were doing. "Very crafty. They do not want this to look too obvious, too definitive in terms of the progress of the engagement. I see what that old fox Louis is doing. Don't count your chickens before they hatch! Ah ha! Well, when he sees my little chick, he shall not be able to resist her for his grandson."

I hope that Monsieur Ducreux did not understand. For as the "little chick" who does understand German, I, for one, found it most discomforting.

March 11, 1769

Monsieur Ducreux did understand! I was mortified. But he was so kind. He said, "Do not blush, Archduchess, or

36

I shall not have enough crimson left for your dress. Fear nothing, you are the loveliest creature I have ever painted. You are so young, so fresh." He shooed Monsieur Larseneur away when he came in with a basket of hairpieces and a tub of powder. "Non! Non! None of that. Would you powder the blossoms of the cherry tree? Would you tint the *muguets* that spring from the earth after the last snows of winter? Are you crazy?" Then he entertained me with delightful stories of how wonderful the woods around Versailles are and the lovely riding, especially in the spring when the wild bulbs first start to emerge and the millions of snowdrops pop from the earth. Oh, it sounds heavenly. I really like Monsieur Ducreux very much. He seems so artistic in every way. He paints as well with words as he does with his brush.

April 5, 1769

So sorry, dear diary, that I haven't written but I have been so ill these past three weeks. Everyone came down with the chest catarrh, including Mama. Now she has us all on a strict regimen in which we are required to drink donkey's milk at least once a day. She says donkey's, or ass's, milk is much better than cow's milk when one has a phlegmy chest congestion. She suggested this, not the doctor. Mama says that if she were not the Empress she would be a doctor! She says this all the time, even in front of Herr Doktor Kreinetz. He is used to it. He just smiles. I don't think there is anything that Mama thinks she could not do. How often I hear her sigh and say if she only had the time — meaning if she were not the Empress of the Holy Roman Empire. I shall make a list of the things Mama says she would be if she were not Empress:

·doctor
·opera singer
·horse trainer
·apothecary
·gunnery sergeant

She actually said that is what she would have liked to be in 1756 when The Monster invaded Saxony and she was examining the axle system of a new gun carriage. If she were not Empress, she told the troops, she would love to "wheel this gun about and blow the behind off The

Monster!" This endeared her to the soldiers and gave rise to a very rude rhyme shouted by them in the battlefield:

Bend over, Freddy of Prussia
Let the Empress take aim
Your butt will fly to Russia
Your brains to sunny Spain

My mother!

April 6, 1769

I am back posing for Monsieur Ducreux. I was too sick for the last weeks so he just worked on the dress part of the painting and the background. It shall be finished in another week, he thinks, and then be sent off to France. I hope they like me. I hope the Dauphin thinks I am pretty. I tried very hard to have a sweet expression and a kind look in my eye. While Ducreux paints, I think of ways that I might make the Dauphin happy. I think of little jokes and rhymes I can share with him. I wonder if I would ever have enough nerve to tell him the soldiers' rhyme about Mama. It is so funny but I think I would blush too much. I mean, I cannot imagine ever saying the word *butt* to the man who will be my husband. Oh my goodness, I turn red right here in the privacy of my chamber even thinking about it.

April 17, 1769

Have not written much lately. Between celebrating Easter and all the confusion of getting ready to move the Court to Schönbrunn there has hardly been a minute. Even my lessons with Abbé de Vermond and Dance Master Noverre have ceased for now. The Abbé marvels at my progress and then gives a wink and says, "I think your little friend has helped." By "little friend" he means you, dear diary, and that is exactly what you have been to me these past several months. What a blessing it was the first day the Abbé brought you into my apartments and handed you to me. You are the one with a lock, but you have allowed me to unlock my heart and my deepest thoughts.

My portrait is on its way to France, to the Court of Versailles. I tremble every time I think of it. What will he, the Dauphin, think of me? What if I am not pretty enough? What if my eyes appear dull or harsh to him? I thought the portrait a good likeness, but how is one to judge her own face? I mean, I know not what Louis Auguste looks like. He might be the most handsome young man on earth. He might look like a god from Mount Olympus. And the women of the French Court are supposed to rival Aphrodite. Yes, that is what they said about King Louis's last "good friend," Madame Marquise de Pompadour. I might look like just a poor Viennese church mouse.

Oh dear, I am so nervous. I just pray to God every night that the Dauphin won't be disappointed, but if an official marriage proposal does not come within the next month, I shall be frantic with worry. And what will Mama do? I suppose she will make me an Abbess as she did my oldest sister, Anna, who lives in a convent in Prague. Mama also made Elizabeth an Abbess of a convent in Innsbrück. They do not have to live there. They just visit occasionally. This, however, is what happens to Archduchesses for whom no husbands can be found.

April 25, 1769
Schönbrunn Palace

We are here at last. Is there anything with more tumult and confusion than when the Court moves? We all must go to bed for the better part of the next day once we get here, except for Mama, of course, who met with some ministers. In all, there are more than one thousand people in our retinue when we go to Schönbrunn. The Empress's carriage alone is accompanied by twenty-three others to carry her Ladies-in-Waiting, the maids, the Master of the Plate, meaning her coin and silver, the Master of the Palace Linen, the apothecary. Then there are four kitchen coaches specially designed to carry various utensils and foodstuffs, in addition to the usual courtiers, trumpeters, pages, postilions, and guards on horseback. Oh yes, and a special coach for Father Confessor and the chaplain and then eighteen other coaches with our baggage and other provisions, including two for musical instruments.

April 27, 1769

It is so lovely to be at Schönbrunn. Everything is so much easier here. We are allowed picnics every day. We go just with Hans and Lulu. None of Mama's Ladies-in-Waiting are required. However, I invited the Abbé to our first one yesterday and Titi talked Elizabeth into coming. Elizabeth wears white veils at Schönbrunn to cover her face instead of the dark ones that she wears in Vienna. I think she likes the sun to shine through and warm her. I was watching her today as she sat on the tapestry in Lark Meadow. That is what we call one of our favorite places for picnics because there are so many larks. She has a perfect figure and perfect posture. Through the veil I could see her profile. It is far more beautiful than mine. Her face is exquisite. They say that we Habsburgs have a slightly protruding lower lip. It is true, except for Elizabeth. And her eyes are the color of violets. A lark began to sing and she took my hand and said, "Listen, Antonia! Listen!" Then she tapped out the rhythm of the lark's song on my palm. I looked at her and through her veil I could see that she was smiling. She looked happy in a way that I have never seen anyone look happy in my life.

April 29, 1769

Another picnic today and horseback riding. Mama did not go with us so I rode astride and not sidesaddle. Mama, who has always ridden astride herself, suddenly says that I should not. I think this is something the French have suggested. It is ridiculous and one's balance is so much better astride. I went with Ferdinand and Hans and Lulu (she rode sidesaddle of course) and my brother Max, who is just a year younger. Max is a fantastic rider. We like to race.

May 5, 1769

Mama is furious with me. I think I have never seen her so angry. Max and I went riding again today and raced through a sparse woods that we love and then out the other side where there is a creek. Well, this year the water was much higher in the creek than we expected and my petticoats were soon drenched, and I was splattered with mud from head to toe. When we came back into the courtyard, Mama was standing there with a delegation of gentlemen. I could see from their dress that they were from the Court of Versailles, for their livery was gold and pale blue, the same colors as your cover, dear diary. I got this awful sinking feeling. For a moment I thought maybe no one would recognize me since I was so mud-splattered and, of course, astride on the horse.

I was bade approach and I did and slipped out of the saddle. Mama looked like a stone statue. I curtsied, and a blob of mud fell from my neck. "Antonia," Mama said, "you of course remember Ambassador Durfort and his councilors." I was mortified. "I think you had best excuse yourself and bathe," she said, her voice like ice.

Oh, dear Lord, have I ruined everything? How shall I ever make this up to Mama? I feel terrible. There is a note from Mama that I am to come to her apartments tomorrow morning.

May 6, 1769

Well, I have seen Mama. It was worse than I could have imagined in ways that I had never imagined. Mama did not scream or rant — and she has been known to do that before. No, she was still and silent. She just glared. She did not say a word for a full four minutes, I think, and she had dismissed her Ladies-in-Waiting and her guard! I have never known her to do this. Indeed, I had never in my life been alone with Mama until that moment. It felt very odd. After she dismissed them, she just continued to stare. And the minutes stretched on and on. Then she made two small gestures, but she made sure I was noticing. She twisted her wedding ring on her left third finger, and then she twisted the diamond ring of the Holy Roman Empire on the finger next to it. With these two small gestures I knew that I had failed in the most sacred tasks that had been put to me. I had endangered my marriage prospects and endangered the Empire. It was almost as if in these few seconds I could feel the hot breath of The Monster on all our backs. Then Mama said, "Get out!" and the words scalded the air.

May 7, 1769

I went to Father Confessor today. I wanted him to give me more rosaries to say than he did. I was hoping he would make me dress in scratchy wool and eat no meat, just por- ridge with no sugar for a week. But he didn't. I must seek my own penance, I guess.

May 10, 1769

I have read the book of meditations Mama gave me for my last birthday. I have skipped two picnics. I have sat in the chapel for nearly ten hours over the past two days, and I refuse to eat meat.

May 11, 1769

Elizabeth came to my apartments today. She brought a plate of meat and a bowl of strong broth and a glass of ass's milk. When I saw the ass's milk, I knew Mama had to have had a hand in this.

Elizabeth behind those veils sees and understands more than anyone in the Court. She spoke softly. Her words stirred the veil like a summer breeze. "You want to wear a scratchy gown. You want a whip to beat yourself like the monks. You want only bread and water, and in that way you feel you can make it up to Mama. But Mama is so clever. She realizes that by saying nothing and giving you no penance this is the worst punishment of all. She is saying that there is no way you can make this up. And besides, she would never let you scratch your lovely skin with coarse material or not eat meat for fear the bloom will go out of your cheeks and then . . ."

And then I added, "I would be too ugly for the Dauphin." The veil moved slowly up and down as Elizabeth nodded her head. "I understand," I said.

Then she surprised me. For she said, "You don't understand everything, Antonia." I asked her what she meant. Then Elizabeth said the most astonishing thing. So I am writing every word down here as best as I can remember. "Mama has the power to punish you in this manner only insofar as you let her. Mama is skillful at filling people's minds and bending their will to hers. But do not let her punish you in this way. What you did, yes, it was wrong. But it was not a sin, mortal or venial. She told Father Confessor not to give you many rosaries or severe penance because she knew she could do better. But Father Confessor would not have in any case. Father Confessor knows what is God's domain and he knows what is Austria's. You have sinned only against . . ."

"Austria," I started to say.

But Elizabeth cut me off as sharply as I have ever heard her speak in my life. "No! Mama's idea of Austria." In that moment it was as if I could see straight through Elizabeth's veils, and what I saw was a woman completely free, free of Mama, free of Austria, free of empires and husbands and filled only with her own music and love of God. If people, especially women, knew the secret of Elizabeth, she would be the most envied woman in the Empire, in Europe, in the world!

May 14, 1769

I picnic now. I go to chapel one hour each day instead of five. I practice my harp diligently and have asked Elizabeth to help, and I spend many minutes several times a day trying to concentrate on what Elizabeth said: not letting Mama fill my mind. This is difficult, for Mama is a strong presence even when she is not nearby. One has to really concentrate to get Mama out of one's thoughts. I do not seek to be defiant of Mama, but I do seek to have my own thoughts and not let her will so completely invade my nature. It is after all <u>my</u> nature and not Mama's. People have always said that I am much like dear Papa in spirit, but I must be something more, too. Something that is just me, and only me.

May 19, 1769

A masked ball tonight. Funny, I have not thought once about trying to persuade Elizabeth to attend. Titi wonders why, for this was to be our big project. It is hard for me to explain to her. She is so young. But now that I have seen how complete, how happy Elizabeth is, trying to force her to go to a masked ball seems rather silly.

May 20, 1769

The ball was beautiful. They moved the dancing plat-forms into the rose gardens, which were illuminated with huge torches, and they tinted the water pink in the foun-tains. I danced until I thought my feet would drop off. Master Noverre pranced up to me with his beaked eagle mask and whispered that the French delegation was en-chanted with my gavotte. I have not truly mastered all the complicated figures of French dances. These are much more difficult than our simple Austrian dances. However, he complimented me on how cunning it was of me to add a *tendu* at the finish, which revealed my ankle. I didn't even know I had revealed my ankle. It was certainly unintentional. I hope Mama didn't see it. She would have been angry. It is just that Titi and I have had much ballet instruction since arriving at Schönbrunn and I guess it must somehow creep into my dancing. A *tendu* is an extension of the leg and of the foot. The foot must have the toes pointed, of course. I just seem to do it.

May 23, 1769

I went riding for the first time since The Incident. I did not ride astride and I did not gallop through mud. And it was not nearly as much fun.

May 27, 1769

Mama has gone back to Vienna for a few days. She always does this in the summer for she likes to visit Papa's tomb. She cannot bear to be away from it for too long. So I went riding astride today but did not get mud-splattered. It was still fun.

May 28, 1769

Rode astride and got muddy. Even more fun.

May 29, 1769

Mama returned today. Rode sidesaddle through a meadow.

June 2, 1769

My brother Leopold arrived today with his wife, Maria Luisa of Spain. Their little boy Francis is enchanting. He looks like a little fat cherub, all rosy and golden. And he smiles all the time. This is amazing to Titi and me because Maria Luisa never smiles and is the most severe, somber person I have ever met.

June 4, 1769

Little Francis came running down the long corridor with his Nursey chasing him and spotted Titi and me at the ballet barre with Master Noverre. He charged right in and went up to the barre. He could barely reach it, but he started doing exactly what we were doing. Master Noverre was delighted. I think the child is a genius. He followed everything we did and pointed his toes and held up his arms for *port de bras*.

June 5, 1769

Little Francis is like a beam of sunshine darting around the palace. Mama, too, is enchanted with him. She gave him a puppy and a pony, and he loves to crawl up onto her lap and play with the emerald pendant she often wears. Do you know I cannot remember ever sitting in Mama's lap? She must have been so busy with all sixteen of us, although three had died young. Maximillian, Ferdinand, and I are just one year apart. There would have hardly been time to dandle us on her lap. I do remember sitting on Papa's lap. Papa had not nearly so much to do, however. For although Papa had the title of Emperor, he was not the one who ruled through birthright. That is Mama. Papa had been the Duke of Lorraine. Lorraine was a duchy, or province. Although it is now part of the Austrian Empire, it sits in the northeast corner of France. Very inconvenient, for it made it a borderland that has always been fought over between France and Austria, and Prussia and Spain, too. It was Mama and Papa's marriage that set off a terrible fracas that is now called the Austrian War of Succession. The French wanted this horrid Bavarian lout to rule and be Emperor. The only way Mama could be Empress was to give Lorraine to Poland with the agreement that when Papa died, it would go back to France. And so it did, in 1766. Now if I marry the Dauphin and then become Queen at least I shall be ruling over what once belonged to Papa. That will make me most happy, and I hope from heaven Papa will smile down, too.

June 7, 1769

Mama has been having me visit her every morning for twenty minutes. Lulu accompanies me and we go over the etiquette of the Court of Versailles. I think as I see Mama reading the charts that Lulu has prepared that she sometimes thinks it is too much herself. Her eyebrow shot up this morning. "What is this? There is the Lady of Honor and then there is the tirewoman and the first *femme de chambre* and then there is the undertirewoman and a wardrobe woman? All that to get dressed?"

Mama especially does not like the part where the *femmes de chambre* have the right to sell the old discarded clothes of the Dauphine or the Queen and that they can have, as needed, all the wax candles of the bedchamber and card room for their own use. I asked Mama why not, and she answered simply, "It gives them too much power over others beneath them; they can buy and sell their influence this way. Not good. I would never permit it."

Indeed, I had the distinct feeling that Mama felt the whole system was too elaborate and much too costly. "Two Ladies of the Bath! Ridiculous! You've been bathing yourself since you were six years old." Then she paused. "Of course, if you insist on riding through muddy creeks, it might take four Ladies of the Bath!" and I thought I saw a little twinkle in Mama's eye and a twitch at the corner of her lip. But she whisked out of the room so suddenly I couldn't tell. But I do believe that this is the first joke Mama has ever made. I think it's wonderful. Mama made a joke!

June 13, 1769

Oh my God! It has come at last — the marriage proposal!
King Louis XV's personal envoys arrived this morning. I
was called immediately to Mama's summer house, the
Gloriette, where she works on the hottest days. I did not
know what I was being called for. Indeed, I thought maybe
Maria Luisa had told Mama about our picnic and I was to
be reprimanded for hill rolling! But as soon as I set foot in
the cool marble receiving room, Mama was out of her
chair behind her desk and running toward me. She
crushed me to her bosom and whispered, "Antonia, you
are to be married! You are to be the Queen of France!" Her
cheeks were wet with tears and soon mine were, too! She
took me immediately to the chapel, where we both fell on
our knees and thanked God for this great and good fortune. Mama held my hand tightly all through the prayers
as they were chanted by Father Confessor. So it has all
worked. All of Mama's planning — the lessons, the hair
treatment — all of it has worked. I have come so far in six
months. Dear diary, I write so fluently now. Did you know
that in the past when I was required to write even the simplest of notes, my old governess, Brandy, would first pre-

pare the note in pencil and then I would write over the words in ink? And look at me now. Oh, I think when I am Queen of France I shall probably have to do much writing. Or maybe not. They probably have secretaries who write for you. But maybe I shall be like Mama and write my own letters.

June 14, 1769

People now regard me differently. And most certainly Maria Luisa does. I think she is slightly disappointed. She among others, I believe, never thought the marriage would come to be. But now they all know and their behavior tells the difference. They stop speaking when I come near, just as they do when my mother passes. They take a step back not just in the narrow corridors of Schönbrunn but in the very widest ones. And my teachers, like Noverre and, yes, the Abbé, too, act differently. All except for Lulu. She is still the same dear old Lulu.

June 15, 1769

Mama says we must make a pilgrimage to Mariazellen, a village some miles away. There is a statue of the Virgin in wood and it is believed she brings luck and many children to young married couples. We leave tomorrow and shall stay there in a monastery for a week in retreat where we shall do nothing but pray and fast lightly, which means no meat but fish. No pastries. Just "simple food," as Mama keeps saying. This means thin broths, ass's milk (Mama's favorite for everything), cheeses, and, of course, bread. Perhaps a pear from the monastery orchards.

I think it shall be very boring, as I am not even permitted to write. But that perhaps is good, for if I brought you, dear diary, and Mama and I share a room, well, she might discover you. Even in a monastery my mother could not resist poking her nose into a private diary!

But in all honesty I do not mind going. If this is what Mama wants and she wants it only for my happiness in marriage, then this is the least I can do.

July 5, 1769

Back from Mariazellen. It was not as boring as I thought. Each day we spent many hours praying to the Virgin. Her lovely face has been nearly worn smooth of paint and her expression seems dim. Each day as I looked at her and prayed, I seemed to see her in a new light, and finally in the last days I realized that she indeed did remind me of my sister Elizabeth, for it was as if the years of wear, the thinning of the paint, the smoothing of the wood, dropped a veil of sorts across her face — a veil of tranquility and complete acceptance.

When we were not praying, we helped the nuns with their embroidery. We took walks in the nearby hills, which were sprigged with field flowers, and we drank lots of ass's milk. It was quiet. It was simple and it rests in a corner of my mind like a calm little island.

July 7, 1769

I am being taught a new card game that is becoming very popular at Versailles. Abbé de Vermond says it is a favorite now of King Louis's daughters Adelaide, Victoire, and

Sophie. I am told that the King was much impressed with the pastel Ducreux sent of me. Now I hope they shall send one of the Dauphin. I am so eager to see what my future husband looks like. I know so little about him. However, I do know that his birthday is coming up. He shall be fifteen on August 23. I think I should make a gift for him. Perhaps an embroidered vest. Oh, I could never finish it by then. Maybe something smaller. An embroidered cover for his prayer book. The Dauphin is almost fifteen months older than I am. I shall turn fourteen on November 2. I think this is a nice age difference. Ferdinand of Naples is much older than Caroline. He has a vast amount of wrinkles and many gray hairs, some sticking straight out of his ears. It's rather disgusting.

July 12, 1769

The *poupées* from France arrived today. They are the little fashion dolls that show how the various dresses look when worn. They are absolutely charming and stand about one foot high. One is just for undergarments — chemises, shifts, underpetticoats, petticoats, corsets, and hoops. But the dresses themselves are what are the most amazing. The *modiste,* or designer, for these new fashions is a young woman named Rose Bertin, and she has made the most extraordinary creations. I love them all. I want them all, and these are only her designs for the early spring season at Versailles. The panniers have grown even wider, and this allows for more decorations and flounces and lace frills. The necklines are much lower, and I must say these dollies have more bosom than I do. And then there are the most beautiful flower-decorated ribbons called *échelles* that tumble down the fronts of the dresses over the stomacher. The stomacher is an inset triangle that goes from the neckline of the dress down over the stomach and helps the waist appear thinner.

My favorite gown, however, was one called a *polonaise.* It is really more of an overdress or coat dress with a skirt that opens from the waist down and is drawn up to show the petticoats. Mama thought it was scandalous. But I loved it and it looks so comfortable. I ordered two *polonaises* and two *robes à la Créole,* which is supposedly fashioned after gowns worn by French ladies in the Americas. It is very simple, almost the weight of a chemise, and is caught at the waist with a large sash. And then I ordered several of the huge pannier gowns and numerous mantles and cloaks. The wedding is set for May and Madame Bertin has already begun on my wedding dress and a *poupée* will be coming next month. I think the dress is to be of white satin brocade with diamonds. The *poupée*, of course, will have fool's diamonds. Oh, this is all so exciting! I can hardly stand it. I am counting the days.

July 15, 1769

With the *poupées* came a long letter from a Countess de Noailles. She is to be my Lady of Honor. The letter was very kind. She said she thought she would take the opportunity to explain to me some of the etiquette pertaining to fashion and dressing, since I had the *poupée* before my eyes. And then, unbelievably, there were fifteen pages of closely written rules and regulations concerning fashion and dressing. How shall I ever remember them all? An exceedingly stupid one comes to mind right now: lappets, which are two long flaps on either side of a headdress and are usually worn pinned up, are always to be loosened and left hanging when receiving people in the state apartments. No one ever lets their lappets hang in Court here. They are such a nuisance. Mama always has hers pinned up. They get into the ink pots when she is writing. Although the Countess's tone is most friendly, I hope that she is not too strict about all of these rules of etiquette.

July 18, 1769

I could not help but think what a wonderful summer this has been — picnics, horseback riding, balls. They say that at Versailles a Princess must be accompanied by no less than four of her Ladies-in-Waiting, a chair carrier, and a valet. And that when a Princess is on her way to the King's suite, she is required to be carried only as far as the guard's room and then alight there before entering the presence of the King. No one carries anyone around here. We do not even have such chairs.

July 19, 1769

These disturbing thoughts about etiquette occupy my mind more and more. Almost once a week it seems new papers arrive concerning the various rituals of the Court. Now one has come about card playing. I don't really play cards that well to begin with. But now I am required to understand that only a Lady-in-Waiting can hand the cards directly to me and not a Lady of the Chamber. I am trying my best to learn all this. I must say, Lulu makes it as nice as possible and sometimes funny.

Despite all this etiquette I must learn for Versailles, I am determined to enjoy the rest of the summer and the special freedom I find here at Schönbrunn. Titi and I went wading in the fountains in our nightrails last night. It was so hot. So we just decided to do it. I wager that I should never be permitted this at Versailles — even if I were Queen and commanded it. This is probably a terrible thought to commit to paper. However, I must say it, although Mama would be furious: but what is the point of being the Queen of France if one cannot wade barefoot in one's nightclothes?

July 24, 1769

The wedding dress *poupée* arrived today. It is the most splendid gown. It is white brocade with stripes of diamonds. The hoops are immense. There was included a note from the *modiste,* Madame Rose Bertin, saying that she designed this gown with the Hall of Mirrors at

Versailles in mind. It is through this Hall that the wedding procession shall pass on its way to the Royal Chapel. More than five thousand seats are to be installed so that spectators may view us. Madame Bertin writes ". . . and the four thousand diamonds that are right now being sewn onto your gown shall appear as forty million in the Hall of Mirrors! You shall be, Your Highness, the most magnificent creature on earth!"

Mama read this and made a little face, then muttered, "I'm glad they're paying for it." I blushed. How can Mama think of cost at a time like this?

July 27, 1769

The heat has been terrible. It is nearly impossible to sleep. Titi and I went out again tonight to wade and you'll never guess who joined us. Mama! Titi and I were so frightened when we saw her coming. She was with one of her Ladies of the Chamber and wore a great cape over her chemise. Then she spoke up. "This is the best idea of the whole summer." She sat down on a bench, took off her shoes, unrolled her stockings, walked over, and climbed into the fountain. She let her chemise drag through the water.

"Ooh, Bissy!" she called to her Lady of the Chamber, "Come in. It's the best!" Then under her breath she whispered to us, "She never will. She's such a fearful thing." And Bissy didn't. But Mama and Titi and I waded about and Mama told us she used to do this when she was young. I noticed, for the moon was full and the light was good, that Mama has grown quite stout. Her wet chemise clung to her calves, which looked like large hams.

Then we sat by the side of the fountain's pool and looked up at the stars. Mama knows so much. She pointed out several constellations, and she tried to explain to me how ships can navigate by tracking their movement against that of the stars. But I could not understand it. It seemed like very complicated mathematics. I have been taught very little of mathematics. I wondered why Mama knows so much about such things and I so little. Then she said, "Well, that was so refreshing that I think I am ready for more work! Bissy, bring the red lacquer box to my chamber and I shall read a few of those papers before I retire. Good night, Antonia. Good night, Theresa." And she lumbered off in the moonlight. Her immense shadow stretched clear across the terrace. And I thought I heard her muttering to herself that rude rhyme about Freddy. You know the one:

Bend over, Freddy of Prussia
Let the Empress take aim
Your butt will fly to Russia
Your brains to sunny Spain

I wonder if Mama is planning another war. I hope not. At least not before my wedding.

July 28, 1769

I was called to the Gloriette for a meeting with Mama this morning. Usually when I come I stand throughout the meeting, as do all of Mama's subjects, but this time she ordered a chair fetched for me and placed it on the other side of the desk. No one except my brother Joseph, who now rules with Mama as Emperor, ever sits opposite the Empress in her offices. This is most unusual. But it suddenly struck me why. Last night Mama and I had waded together, splashed with bare calves and dripping nightrails in the fountain. It was fun and very frivolous. This is Mama's way of saying that my position is changing. That perhaps we can do such antics very privately here at Schönbrunn but that — yes, I saw it in the way in which she fixed me in the glint of her eye. That said it all — *We are rulers, Antonia. Majesty is required.* And then she really did say it in so many words.

"Antonia, when you go to France, you shall no longer be known as Antonia but as Marie Antoinette. Antonia is the name of a girl. Marie Antoinette is the name of a Queen."

P.S. I do not think Mama regrets wading in the fountain pool. Mama is not built for regret. It is not part of her. I think she just wants me to understand the difference between this kind of behavior, which must be kept private, and the conduct of a Queen, which is for the public.

August 1, 1769

We received new dispatches today concerning dining etiquette and protocol. And I am beginning to wonder if there can be any time for a private life at Versailles. It seems that it is customary for the French Royal Family to take their evening supper in public several days of the week and that people are admitted to the galleries above the dining salon so they might look down and watch the King, his daughters, and his grandchildren dine! There can be up to one thousand people watching. I think this might be upsetting to my digestion. I turned to Schnitzel, who was with me in my chamber, and said, "Dear Schnitzy, how would you feel about having to eat in front of all those people?" He actually barked. I took it as "I wouldn't like it."

August 2, 1769

Titi came to me very concerned today. She said that Mama has instructed her to call me Marie Antoinette and she finds it very uncomfortable. She said it is like a shoe that doesn't fit. So I asked, doesn't fit you or me? And she said, "Neither one of us." It is much too long a name for such a short person, she said. So I told her to call me Antonia in private and use Marie Antoinette only when the Empress is present. "But what about Tony?" she asked, for she often calls me Tony. I assured her she could still do that in private. I might have added that I hope she does indeed call me that in private, for it is almost as if I can see my private world disappearing, simply melting away, and what shall be left? And <u>who</u> shall be left? Will I recognize this Marie Antoinette, Dauphine, wife of Louis Auguste Bourbon, future Queen of France? Who is she?

August 3, 1769

Mama has decided to give a grand ball after our return to Vienna. We go back to the Hofburg Palace in September, and she says it will take a month to prepare for the ball. She has sent a dispatch to the Court of Versailles to see if the *modiste* Madam Rose Bertin could create a wonderful gown for me.

August 4, 1769

I shall say it outright. I dread the end of summer. This is perhaps the last time I shall ever be at Schönbrunn. Every time we do something, I think this is one of the last times I might do this — the last time we shall all picnic together, the last time I shall race my horse through the woodlands.

August 27, 1769

It has been more than three weeks since I have written. You see, dear diary, we put on a play and my toe became infected from all the dancing I did in it. The infection crept up my foot and my ankle, and my leg began to swell. Indeed, if I thought Mama's calf looked like a ham that night when we were wading, my calf looked like a bigger one. I was beset with fever and even became delirious. I have been bled countless times, and every poultice known in the Empire has been applied to my poor toe. Every day comes an endless stream of Court physicians and apothecaries with new remedies. Well, finally something worked, and the infection began to recede and the swelling went down. As soon as Mama knew I would live, she gave me a scolding such as I have never had. It made the mud-splattering of earlier this summer pale by comparison! She said that we must keep all this a big secret. If the French Court knew that I had been sick, or as she said, so careless, they would break the betrothal contract. She told me how I've put myself, the Empire, and France in mortal danger. Once more I could feel The Monster's

breath at my back. I finally had to close my eyes and pretend I was too weak to listen to any more. But to think, all
this because of a little blister on my toe. Mama finally
took leave. As soon as I heard the door slam, I whispered to
myself, "It was still worth it." I didn't at that time realize
that Elizabeth was in the room. She came over to my bed
and grasped my hand, and for the first time since she con-
tracted the smallpox, Elizabeth raised her veil. Her lovely
violet eyes were bleary with tears. She looked straight into
my eyes and said, "It would not have been worth it if you
had died, sister." Then she smiled that brilliant smile and
I drew her poor pockmarked face to mine and kissed her
all over her dead pitted cheeks.

August 30, 1769

I am still quite weak from my time in bed. And I find myself increasingly nervous about my future. There has yet
to be any letter from Louis Auguste himself or any picture. Maybe if I could see his face it would ease my worries. I might know that I am heading toward a friend. The
word *husband* to me does not have much meaning, really.

Husband, wife — they seem like words Mama thinks up to secure her alliances.

When Caroline went to marry the King of Naples, I felt so alone, so abandoned, but it was after she left that I became closer to Elizabeth. I have made a true friend of my sister. But I shall in some months have to leave her. It seems like too much of life is saying good-bye. It would be so much easier if I thought there was the chance of a true friend waiting for me in France.

September 3, 1769

I am so stupid. I complain that Louis Auguste has never written me, but then again, have I written him? No. It is true that my portrait was sent but that is not the same thing. I am going to write Louis Auguste a letter. I am so much better at letter writing than I was a year ago before I started keeping you, dear diary. I am going to start working on it now. It might take me a few days. And of course tomorrow we leave, as the Court returns to Vienna.

So much confusion. I hardly had any time to try writing my letter. But here is my first attempt — actually it is my second. I am going to copy it out here for practice.

My Dear Louis Auguste,
It is with great warmth that I write you. I am so pleased to be coming to France to become your wife, the Dauphine. I hope that I shall be a wonderful wife to you as well as a wonderful friend. I hope that we shall have many good times together. I am told you love to hunt. Well, I love to ride. I can ride astride or sidesaddle, whichever you think is most fitting. I like to play cards. I like to dance. I am not much of a reader, but I am trying to encourage the reading habit in myself, as I feel it is valuable. I love planning and giving plays. It is something that I would enjoy at Versailles.

I hope that you will find the time to write me and tell me some of the things that you enjoy. If you enjoy something that I know not about, I shall attempt to learn it. I want to share everything with you and we shall through this become great companions.

Faithfully yours,

Marie Antoinette

September 10, 1769

I sent off the letter today through the regular dispatch that goes to Versailles once every ten days. I like thinking about my little letter traveling across the Empire to the border of France, through rutted roads, into valleys, across rivers.

September 11, 1769

I am furious! I feel like a fool. For an entire day I had been thinking about my small letter to Louis Auguste traveling across the Empire to France. Well, guess where it went? To Mama. She called me in this morning to discuss the Grand Ball for October. The new *poupée* has arrived for my gown. First she let me look at it and get all excited and then, so very casually, she said, "Oh, my dear, and here is the letter you wrote to Louis Auguste. It has my corrections. So if you will recopy it, we shall send it in the next dispatch to Versailles." I was stunned as she handed me the letter. My mouth dropped. She looked at me and said, "Marie Antoinette, that is a most unattractive position for your jaw to be hanging in. Please shut it." I began to shut my mouth and managed to gasp, "Mama . . . ," but she cut me off. "I must say, Marie Antoinette, that your handwriting has improved greatly and your spelling is perfect. You have made great strides with Abbé de Vermond." I took the letter and ran out of the room. Here it is in my diary. I have pasted it in.

To his Royal Highness Louis Auguste, Dauphin
I have wished for a long time to show Your Highness and His Majesty your grandfather my great regard and feelings. I am so pleased with the prospect of our impending marriage and the great alliance for peace it promises to bring to both our countries. It is with utmost sincerity that I can say that I shall honor our marriage with the greatest respect and affection.

I look forward to the day when we can kneel beside each other and take our vows. Please convey to His Majesty your grandfather my most cordial wishes. You are both in my prayers constantly. I remain your very affectionate servant,

Maria Antonia Josepha Johanna, Archduchess

I do not know whether I have the heart to rewrite this letter. It is not me who speaks here. It is all Mama. Pure Mama. And if that is not enough, she gave me a whole sheaf of paper explaining her changes. I would at least have thought she would be pleased that I had signed the letter Marie Antoinette after her instructions that everyone here should begin calling me that, but no. Here is what she wrote. "You must sign yourself by your full Christian name. You are not Marie Antoinette yet! And we want to remind them constantly whom they are marrying and the implications of this marriage."

I want to reply to her, "Yes, Mama. I am not a person. I am not even yet a woman. I am a girl who also happens to be an empire. Empires do not have feelings. Empires do not have interests or hobbies like riding or dancing.

Empires don't go wading. Empires don't make friends, just alliances."

October 11, 1769

I have not written for a month. No heart. I am still feeling most dismal. But the Grand Ball approaches and Elizabeth has spoken sharply to me. So it is for Elizabeth that I am trying to make a good show of things. Almost every day Mama asked me when I was going to rewrite the letter. But I was sullen and often just shrugged my shoulders. Mama has no patience with sulking children. So what did Mama do in this case? She ignored me and wrote the letter herself and signed my name. This of course made me even madder. But now Elizabeth says I must get over it and get on with my life. So I am trying to look cheerful today when I go for the fitting of my gown for the ball. It is beautiful. Made of cloth of silver with teardrop pearls hanging in cascades along the flounces. I have already had many sessions with the hairdresser. He is designing something very special for the ball. It will involve at least two full switches and a dozen braids. Seamstresses are working on the silk flowers for my hair.

October 14, 1769

It has been a month since Mama wrote the letter supposedly from me to the Dauphin, but still no picture has arrived. I do not understand. Abbé de Vermond assures me
that the Dauphin is, in his words, of a "pleasing countenance." I am wondering what that really means. I think
if he were handsome, I mean outright handsome, Abbé
de Vermond would say. I do not really know any grown
men or young men, whom I would say are outright handsome. Wait! Johan, the underkeeper of the menagerie at
Schönbrunn, I think is outright handsome. However, perhaps not, for how can one really be that handsome if he is
of low birth? I would think that impossible. It is an interesting question.

October 17, 1769

The Grand Ball is four days away. A large French delegation is expected. Do not expect me to write until after the
ball. There is too much to be done between hairstyling
and last fittings, and there is an entire new folio of etiquette from Versailles that Mama wants me to read over

with her. Then there are extra sessions with Father Confessor. (Yes, can you believe it, Diary? Prayers are being said now, not exactly for the Grand Ball, but just for things in general.) At least three times a day my presence is demanded in Mama's apartments, or if not that, a note comes from her with some tidbit of advice.

Still no portrait from the Dauphin.

October 23, 1769

How good it feels to get back to you, dear diary. I believe in truth that you shall be my last refuge, my last bit of privacy on earth. I sit at my dressing table to write. Tonight was the Grand Ball. I have dismissed my chambermaids before getting undressed. I shall do it by myself. I need to be alone.

There were over four thousand people there. Although they stood back respectfully, I could sense this pressing toward me. They wanted to see the next Dauphine, the future Queen of France. Every single eye in the Grand Ballroom was fastened on me. I have never been very good in mathematics, but I think that is many thousands, for if there are four thousand people and each person has two eyes, I suppose one just multiples. So that must mean eight thousand eyes.

It was so strange. I felt as if my clothing, my very skin, were being peeled from my bones. I started to tremble at first, but then some odd force seemed to grow within me and I was able to walk through the guests. It was almost as if magically I knew what to say, although I really knew few of the people personally. But words just came to me — a comment about a lady's fan, a remark about the glorious weather, a word here, a word there — not of course too many. One should never be overly familiar, as Mama always says. I quickly grew accustomed to this role of mine. I heard more than once the word *majestic* whispered as I floated by. Yes, I did float. Noverre's lessons are now forever embedded into my very feet.

I look up now into the oval mirror and see barely a trace of the mud-splattered girl tearing through the woodland on her horse, or the barefoot girl wading at Schönbrunn. She is dissolving into the fountain's mists. I have become what Mama set out for me to be. Majestic. A Dauphine and eventually a Queen. Perhaps I am majestic because I am nothing else. I lean forward to peer more closely at my image in my mirror. It is difficult. The wig weighs five pounds, and the gown itself is made of twenty-two yards of silk and has eight pounds of pearls. Yet I float. I am light. I am Mama's dream. Dreams weigh nothing.

October 24, 1769

Mama sent a message that I was to have breakfast with her. This is very rare, for Mama usually signs papers and meets with ministers during her breakfast. She is so deft with her writing that she can eat and write and never drop a speck of porridge on the papers.

She is most pleased with my deportment at the ball. She beamed all through breakfast. I have learned my lessons well, she exclaimed. And now that she realizes how well, and what a quick learner I am, she has ordered that I have even more lessons!

This, of course, sounds like nonsense to an ordinary person, but it is typical of Mama. She pushes and pushes and pushes. I do not know how there will be enough hours in the days for all that she plans for me to do. But she insists as the wedding is barely six months away. Abbé de Vermond is to increase by one hour the time devoted to

French civilization and history. Lulu is to increase by two hours my etiquette lessons. Presently I only have gambling instruction once a week, but Mama thinks twice is needed to show me the finer points of the game *cavagnole*, for she has found out that this is the favorite of Sophie, Victoire, and Adelaide, King Louis XV's daughters.

The best part is that I am to go to the Spanish Riding School every day. Mama wants me to learn the French way of sitting in the saddle from the riding master. Not sidesaddle. It is just a manner of riding astride where the weight is farther back. This I shall love. But goodness knows when I shall have time to write in your pages, dear diary.

October 29, 1769

All Hallows' Eve is nearly here. We always have bonfires and games. It is so much fun. But Mama insists that these are children's games and that I can no longer participate. I begged Mama. I asked, can't I be a child for only two more days? I am still thirteen for three more days. On November 2, I turn fourteen.

November 3, 1769

My birthday has come and gone. Mama gave me a diamond necklace that had belonged to her grandmother
Margarita Theresa of Spain, the wife of the Emperor
Leopold I. Maria Luisa, my brother Leopold's wife, is upset, I can tell. She feels that it should have come to her, for
after all she is married to Leopold's namesake. I would
give it to her in a minute. To tell you the truth, what I
would have much preferred would have been a letter from
Louis Auguste for my birthday — but nothing has arrived, absolutely nothing.

Later: I was thinking about how much I wanted a letter
or just something from Louis Auguste and I began to cry,
just softly, and suddenly Lulu appeared in my chamber.
She saw that I was upset. It only took one look from my
dear Lulu for me to burst into a flood of tears. I told her
everything. She folded me into her arms and whispered
soft words to me. And then she said in another voice, "I
have a plan, Antonia." The change of the tone in her voice
stopped my crying.

Now listen to this. Lulu knows one of the couriers from
Versailles who makes the monthly trips. She says I should

write my letter and she is sure she could sneak it into the pouch without Mama knowing. She says the courier owes her a favor. I was perplexed and said, "He does?" She nodded, and I asked, "Why?" And she said, "None of your business," and tweaked my nose.

I am happy once more. Tomorrow I shall rewrite the letter that Mama made all the crossings out on and send it just the way I want it.

November 8, 1769

The letter is truly on its way. I would have certainly heard about it from Mama by now, I think, if she had intercepted it. But Lulu assures me she didn't. Now I must wait.

November 9, 1769

I am enjoying very much my riding lessons with Riding Master Herr Francke. The French method is slightly different. One rides a bit more back in the saddle and, when taking low jumps, thrusts one's feet forward. I love riding in the Riding Hall. There is nothing quite like it. The ceilings soar, and light pours in through the arched windows

in the upper galleries. Then there are dozens of chandeliers. I ride my silvery horse through a shower of sun
drops. And Herr Riding Master Francke is the kindest,
most gentle of men. I love to hear him talk to the horses.
He presses his mouth right to their ears and scratches their
muzzles. And when he speaks to me, he looks straight into
my eyes and he says, "Lovely Archduchess," — he always
addresses me as "Lovely Archduchess" — and then he
goes on and says, "When you pull on the reins to tuck
Cabriole's head in, you do it in a steady, firm motion.
Never a jerk. He is your friend. You are taking a walk, a
stroll with a friend, and you are guiding him along the
most beautiful path. Your good, strong, intelligent hands
will make the path beautiful."

This is what I love about the riding lessons. Everything
is at one time very simple and direct, but in another way
very mysterious. If you jerk your hands, the horse will toss
his head and fight you. It is as if the horse reads your
mind. The horse and you are absolute partners. And Herr
Riding Master Francke seems to be able to explain this
partnership in the loveliest and clearest language. If I had
my way, I would take riding lessons every day all day long

and forget the dancing, the gambling, and definitely the etiquette and the French history.

November 10, 1769

Days when I do not ride are so boring, except of course those moments when I think about my letter to Louis Auguste traveling across Austria. I wonder if it is yet approaching Munich? Maybe in another few days it will reach the Rhine River. That is exciting, for then the letter shall be practically at the French border. But I cannot think about that too much. It shall drive me mad.

November 13, 1769

Almost immediately after I rose yesterday, a message from Mama came. I was to go to her apartments and have my mouth examined by the Royal Dentist. This perplexed me for there is absolutely nothing wrong with my teeth, as far as I can tell. No toothaches, no cracked teeth. But Mama says it will not do to send a bride off with dental problems that might appear later. The dentist examined me and said my teeth were nearly perfect. They spoke briefly of filing one down but thankfully decided against it. He told the apothecary a recipe for tooth polish that will take the stain from one of my lower teeth. Mama nodded approvingly and asked if we will be rid of the stain by May 17. So I asked Mama if that is the official day that I would be married, and Mama told me that I actually would be married in April by what she calls *proxy*. This was a term I had never heard before. It means a substitute. In other words, someone will stand in for Louis Auguste and on his behalf repeat the marriage vows. It will be Ferdinand who does this. So I guess it doesn't matter if this stupid tiny little yellow stain on a tooth that is hardly visible does not fade by April, because Ferdinand is not Louis and Ferdinand is used to my teeth and wouldn't ever care anyway. Cleanliness is not one of Ferdinand's strong points.

Oh, for heaven's sake, a messenger has just arrived from Mama's apartments and my presence is again required!

November 17, 1769

Elizabeth invited me down to her apartments for hot chocolate this evening after supper. We had such a cozy time. She encouraged me to talk about my riding. So I told her all my feelings and what a wonderful teacher Herr Francke is. And how I wish I could take more riding lessons than the three times a week I do now. Suddenly behind the veil I detected a sparkle in Elizabeth's eyes. "I have an idea, Antonia. Here is what you must do, and I promise you Mama will let you have more riding lessons." She said that I must go to Mama and tell her how much I am learning from riding. "You must tell her, Antonia, that you do not learn just about horses and riding in these lessons but indeed about statecraft and power and how to control yourself and other things that are stronger than you. You must say that horsemanship is the perfect metaphor for ruling and governing."

And I said, "What's a metaphor, Elizabeth?" She seemed surprised that I did not know this. She said it is a "figure of speech" in which one kind of thing, one idea, is used to explain another; thus statecraft is explained through horsemanship and controlling horses and riding them. I asked her if it was a kind of substitution. She said similar, but not exactly the same. Then I asked if it is like a proxy marriage. And she frowned and said "No" very sharply. I think I am beginning to understand.

November 20, 1769

It worked! I told Mama about my lessons with Herr Francke. I told her about reining in and how one must do it gently but firmly and know just when to give the horse its head and on and on. And she said at the end of my talk, "Well, Marie Antoinette, I see you learn more in the riding ring than in the schoolroom. I think we must increase these lessons. I shall talk to Herr Francke immediately."

November 25, 1769

Thank heavens I have my riding lessons five days a week now. If not for that, I would be driven crazy. Every day new couriers and new diplomats arrive from Versailles. I would think that by this time my letter has reached Louis Auguste. Now I must wait. I wonder how long. The Christmas holidays are coming. So this might delay a reply. I shall ask Lulu.

November 27, 1769

I asked Lulu when she thought I might hope for a reply from Louis Auguste. Lulu sighed. She seemed distracted and said she didn't know. Well, when is the earliest? I asked. "Oh, I don't know!" She seemed quite impatient with me. Lulu, who is always so patient! I don't understand.

Later: Lulu came to my apartment to apologize for her shortness with me this morning. She said I should not look for a reply to my letter before Christmas, but she thought by the end of January might be a reasonable time. Then she took my hand and gave it a squeeze and sighed. Ordinarily, I would have been pleased by this. Lulu was her old patient self and calm and reasonable, but I am unsettled. It is the old Lulu but she is different. She has grown painfully thin and her face is drawn. "Are you feeling well, Lulu?" I suddenly asked. She smiled at me, a brittle, unnatural smile — not like Lulu at all. Then she quickly got up from the chair and made an excuse about having to run off. I am worried.

November 30, 1769

I was right! Lulu is not well. A maid of her chamber was sent and told me I would not be having my morning etiquette review with her. We were supposed to begin studying the etiquette of the card room. It all sounds so tedious. *Tedious* is a new word I have learned from Elizabeth. She says I say *boring* too much and tedious is a better word than boring although it means the same thing.

If it weren't for the fact that I was so worried about Lulu, these days would be lovely — no etiquette lessons, and Abbé de Vermond has gone to France for the upcoming holidays, so all I really have to do is have my riding lessons. Titi came this morning and said we really had to start thinking about our Christmas play.

December 8, 1769

I do not really understand Lulu's illness at all. She coughs, yes, but it is not pneumonia or a chest catarrh. She is just very weak and she has much pain in her hip, or it might be her leg. I am not sure but it hurts her to walk. She seems to grow grayer and thinner. When I ask what is wrong with her no one tells me. They do not seem to want to speak of it and I, of course, dare not ask Lulu herself. But I wish I knew. It is awful to just see her withering away like a flower going dry, losing its petals. Lulu was always so pretty. She had lovely sparkling gray eyes with a hint of green, but now they are dull and seem no real color and there is no light in them. The angles of her face have turned sharp. I just don't understand. What else is there to get sick from besides pneumonia, smallpox, and child-birth?

December 10, 1769

I am so mad at Mama. I finally decided I had to ask her what was wrong with Lulu and she lied, I know it. She treated Lulu's illness as if it were nothing, and then she said this awful thing. "Lulu has been your Grand Mistress for only two years. I never realized how attached you have grown." As if there were something wrong with that. I told Abbé de Vermond that I was very upset with Mama. I asked him what was wrong. He looked concerned and told me not to worry, that Mama was probably trying to protect me in some way. Protect me from what? I asked.

They are treating me as if I am a child and yet they are expecting me to be a wife in less than six months' time. I do not understand why they put me in these situations. And my love for Lulu is questioned. I am not expected to love someone I have known for such a "short" time as two years, but I am expected to marry and be wife to someone I have never met. I've never even seen his likeness. I purposely shut my mind now to thoughts of my letter. It is there now. But I shall not torture myself wondering whether Louis Auguste will choose to reply.

Oh, I'm feeling most depressed and vexed these days. Abbé de Vermond has required that I do more practice in sketching and painting. Normally, I would love this. It would be a diversion and so much more pleasant than the etiquette lessons and the memorizing of the endless pamphlets sent from Versailles, but now I just have no heart for sketching. I think I would never mind those silly pamphlets again if I knew Lulu would get better.

December 12, 1769

I am much heartened. I went to visit Lulu today and she seems much improved. She was sitting up in bed. She had a blush on her cheeks and a dim sparkle in her eyes, and she wanted to know all I was doing. So I told her not much, seeing as she had been too ill to teach me etiquette. Then she told me that she had heard that I was reluctant to practice my drawing. And she said she did not know why, as my handwriting had improved so much. I think people would truly be astounded with my improvement if they could read you, dear diary. It is amazing when I compare not just the shape of my letters but the ease with which the words flow compared with the first entries I wrote. I brought Schnitzel with me as Lulu always enjoys him so much. He crawled right up on the bed with her and pounced on her lap. I saw her wince a bit. Her hip must still hurt.

Later: Lulu came up with this wonderful idea. She says I should ask Abbé de Vermond if instead of the usual still-life paintings of baskets of fruit and the like which he requires, I might try my hand at drawing the horses at the riding school. Is that not a wonderful idea?

December 13, 1769

I went this morning to draw the horses. I began in the stables. I decided it might be easier at first if I focused just on the head of a horse as it eats from its manger. To draw a horse performing one of its complicated figures would be too difficult. I decided to try the stallion Mars. His head is so large and noble.

December 14, 1769

Drawing Mars is the most challenging thing I have ever done. It has taken hold of my mind, my imagination, completely.

December 17, 1769

My drawing of Mars is really improving. Titi and Ferdinand and Max have been complaining bitterly about no snow. Usually by this time we have enough to go sledding. I don't even care, for now I have decided to do a full portrait of Mars. I stay at the school for two hours after my lesson and watch the Riding Masters exercise Mars on a long line. I have set my goal to make a picture of Mars trotting.

December 20, 1769

Mama has ordered snow brought in from the mountains so we can sled. Titi and Ferdinand and Max are ecstatic. Christmas is almost upon us. Our play is simple this year. Mostly songs, but a tableau vivant of the Nativity passage. Elizabeth plays the Virgin Mary. Ferdinand is Joseph. Mama, my brother Joseph, and I are the Three Kings. Mama says it doesn't matter that she is an Empress or that I am to be the Dauphine. "Rulers are rulers," she says. These are not the only liberties she takes with the Gospel text. Schnitzy and other Court dogs have been transformed into "sheep," thanks to some fuzzy little cloaks the tailors have fashioned for them from wool.

December 21, 1769

Herr Francke says that my drawing has improved my riding. I am doing Piaffe "perfectly," in his words. The horse does not move one bit forward but merely prances or trots in place as he is supposed to do. It seems that drawing the picture has fixed the image in my mind of the horse's feet, and this in some mysterious way makes me sit correctly and give just the right commands at the right pace to the horse.

December 26, 1769

Lulu took part in our Christmas celebration, and although I was very happy, it was something of a shock to see her. Her dress hung on her like the clothes of a scarecrow in the fields we pass on our way to Schönbrunn. Her face seemed all hollows and perhaps worst of all she could not walk without a cane. It was as if she had become an old lady overnight. She had shrunk, and although the hairdresser had fixed many plaits and switches of hair to her head, I could see that beneath them, even her skull seemed smaller, as if its bones rattled beneath the shell of false hair. I think she had overpainted her cheeks in an effort to look like her old self. But there was this new self instead, a self that I almost did not recognize. However, she sat through the St. Nicholas Day feast and then stayed for the entire tableau of our Gospel of St. Luke nativity, and she clapped her hands very merrily when Schnitzy came out wagging his tail and scurried up to the manger to lick the doll who was the baby Jesus.

We all ate too much Christmas torte. It is the best and the most beautiful torte I have ever seen here in the palace. The pastry chef made it specially with me in mind for it was a scene from the Riding Hall. A dozen horses made from marzipan performed atop a wonderful chocolate cake. The pastry chef really outdid himself, and Mama called him out from the kitchens and we applauded and then ate more! And of course, we had already eaten goose and sauerbraten — Mama must always have sauerbraten on a feast table no matter what — and steamed cabbage and dumplings filled with cheese. She loves dumplings above all. There were the usual twelve courses for the Twelve Nights of the Christmas festival season. We shall give our performance once again on Epiphany, or Twelfth Night, the last night before the last day of the twelve. And Cook shall make yet another cake. How he can make a more beautiful one I shall never know!

January 1, 1770

We gave our New Year's gifts this morning. I must admit that I had hoped a letter might come from Louis Auguste. What a perfect gift that would have been. Or even better, perhaps a portrait. I try to imagine what he might look like but I cannot.

I do believe that Titi got the most wonderful gift of all. It is a kind of miniature theater but with moveable parts that illustrate scenes from the Old Testament. Our favorite of course is the Flood and Noah's ark, but most powerful is Moses coming down from the mountain with the Ten Commandments. That is certainly Mama's favorite. She rolls the crank to bring Moses down so often that Titi and I joked that he shall become tired and throw away the Commandments. Mama scowled and called us *anser inscius,* which means "ignorant gosling" in Latin. This is her favorite term for silly, small girl children. Or sometimes she calls us *ridiculus mus,* Latin for "ridiculous mouse."

Just when we were having so much fun playing with this, I was called away, as the French ambassador, Durfort, had arrived. I really did not want to take the time to see him, but then I decided maybe he would like to see the little mechanical theater. "So," I said, "come with me and I shall show you something that you have perhaps never seen!" I took him directly to the nursery room where Titi plays. I think he was enchanted by the little theater.

Madame Bertin has sent the *poupées* for the spring fashions. It is hard to believe that spring will ever come. For now we have so much snow. And when spring does come I shall be in France, gliding down the marble corridors of Versailles as I have been taught to walk. Perhaps I shall be wearing the dress of the little doll that sits in front of me now. She wears a gown of Binche lace. It is lighter than regular lace and is sprinkled with a snowflake design. I like the idea of snowflakes in spring — in fabric, that is, not in the air.

January 7, 1770

Cook did indeed outdo himself. The Twelfth Night cake was not one but several and all replicas of various parts of Versailles! There was the Hall of Mirrors with mirrors made from melted sugar silver. There was the Ambassadors Staircase with a huge flight of chocolate stairs leading up to a sugar replica of the fountain in which two Greek gods frolicked. The walls were so tasty, for they were made from pistachio paste. My favorites, though, were the outdoor parts, the gardens. There was the Orangery with little orange trees hung with sugared drops the shape of oranges. And then my *very* favorite, the Groves, in which the trees had foliage made from spun burnt caramel, so it looked as if it were an autumn day, and the lake known as the Baths of Apollo was made of *crème anglaise* with a waterfall of Royal Frosting pouring into it. I think Mama is considering having a medal made to give to the pastry chef in recognition of his skills.

January 8, 1770

Lulu is ailing once more. I think the Christmas festivities were too much for her. She is back in bed and very weak. Mama sends both of her personal physicians to tend her. Meanwhile every day more dispatches come from Versailles filled with letters concerning the wedding.

January 12, 1770

I was sent for by Mama today and I found her scowling and very cross, snapping at a minister: "What do you mean, Marie Antoinette's name does not come first, not even on the proxy document?" How ridiculous! She was so caught up in the details of the last dispatch from Versailles that she forgot I was there and simply stormed out of the room.

What do I really care whose name comes first? Why should it matter, this sort of etiquette, when Louis Auguste has yet to acknowledge my presence on earth? Still no reply to my letter. I try not to think about it.

January 14, 1770

Every day I hear of a new spat with Versailles. All of it concerning etiquette and protocol and conduct and all those rituals that are part of a great wedding. It is a wonder that any royal person ever gets married. Here is a list of the arguments over the last few days:

1) Whose name should come first on the marriage contract — Mama's, the Empress of Austria (who is giving me away), or Louis, the King of France, who is grandfather of the bridegroom?
2) Who should accompany me to France? (No one of course would ever ask whom I might want.)
3) How many Knights, Ladies-in-Waiting, doctors, secretaries, and laundresses should accompany me?
4) What order should the Austrian and the French nobles who accompany me ride in?
5) What kinds of and how many carriages? Apparently, King Louis has ordered two magnificent traveling carriages built, but who other than myself should ride in them is of great argument at the moment, and I can hardly ride in two at once.

All this seems so utterly stupid and all I really want is a letter or portrait from Louis Auguste. Of course, they never bother me with any of these questions. The only thing I am asked my opinion on are the fashion dolls. Do I want this dress or that dress made from this or that fabric and in what color? The French use fine cloth and have very imaginative names for their fashion colors. Another *poupée* now sits on my bureau by the window. She wears a cambric dress in a soft, fragile white. There is a gray I am particularly fond of called Flea's Head and then a bright green called, of all things, Lovesick Frog. I jest not.

January 19, 1770

Do you remember the *poupée* that I mentioned that stood on my bureau? Well, the oddest thing happened. I woke up this morning and found that she had fallen off the bureau and crashed onto the floor. Her porcelain head smashed into tiny pieces and one arm hung loose on its string from the tiny socket in her shoulder. A wind must have blown in through the loose shutter near the bureau and knocked her down. Poor dear! She looked so terrible, all broken and mangled. It gave me an odd shiver. I think I won't order that dress in the Binche lace.

January 20, 1770

I cannot believe this is happening now. Titi is deathly ill. It is not the smallpox but a very terrible pneumonia. I am thankful it is not the pox, for if it were, they would not let me near her. At least I can go to her chamber and hold her hand. My brother Joseph is there constantly. He is beside himself, for Titi is the image of his dearly beloved first wife, Isabella. She is all he has left of Isabella. I pray to God that she does not die. Dear God, do not take this dear child who has been as much a companion to me as any, despite our age difference.

January 23, 1770

Our dear Titi left us this morning. I feel frozen. It is as if I cannot cry. My tears are as locked as ice in the stream. I look out and I see a frozen world, for it is so bitter that the fountains hang with beards of ice, and the windows are fringed with needles of icicles, and something in me has frozen.

Later: I went to Titi's nursery playroom and looked at the wonderful mechanical theater. I cranked the spindles around until her favorite Old Testament scene came onto the small stage — the ark with the animals entering two by two. I pray that my darling Titi shall be as lovingly cared for by our God as Noah cared for these animals. I have left instructions that the theater scene should never be changed.

January 25, 1770

Two days without Titi. I don't know how I shall ever get used to it. Every day for I do not know how long Titi and I always had our hot chocolate together in the morning. Every time the first snowflake fell, Titi would come running to me. "Will there be enough for sledding, Tony? Can we get Grandmama to bring it in from the high country?" What shall I do without my little Titi? I felt she was like a lovely shadow following me around the palaces, throughout my days, in and out of my classrooms for dancing or music. She was a reminder of all the best things of when I was a child, before this strange time of my betrothal. She made me hope that I could somehow always have a part of me that was young and could sled and play tricks and, yes, be stubborn and bossy and it would do no harm because after all we were just children and not wives or rulers.

Did I mention that I think even Schnitzy realizes that

something has happened to Titi? He scampered off into Titi's playroom this morning and seemed to be searching for her. Then he climbed into my lap, whining and whimpering. There was something almost human about his little moans.

Mama came in just a few minutes ago with a pouch of papers from Versailles to tell me I must meet with her and her ambassador Count Mercy over some important matters concerning the wedding, and I muttered to no one in particular, "It is not fair." She thought I spoke of having to meet with her and Count Mercy and began to lecture me as to my duties and responsibilities. And I interrupted her and said, "No, Mama, I speak of Titi's death. It is not fair." And Mama said, "Nonsense. She was but a child. If a child lives until twelve, it is a miracle. If she dies between twelve and marriage and having children, then it is unfair." I realized then that Mama and I have entirely different views of childhood. Mama thinks that children are not precious because their deaths are so common. They are the disposable part of humanity. And I think just the reverse. Because children are rare, they must be and are the most precious things on earth, because they remind us of the incompleteness of life and are anything but disposable.

We shall not have even a mourning period for Titi. It is not the Austrian custom, as Mama says, to "carry on" about children.

February 7, 1770

I don't feel like writing today. It snowed hard. Snowy days make me miss Titi all the more.

February 10, 1770

I skipped my riding lesson today. Received a severe note from Mama telling me to stop "carrying on" about Titi. I was so mad I drew an ugly picture of Mama with a beard and mustache.

February 11, 1770

I tore up a picture of Mama, then went to Father Confessor and told him what I had done. He gave me one rosary to recite. I thought he would at least direct me toward the carvings of the Stations of the Cross and make me say a prayer at one or two.

February 20, 1770

I went to visit Lulu today. She asked me how things were
going in regard to the wedding. I think she was really asking if I had heard from Louis Auguste, but I did not wish
to tell her the truth about that. So instead I told her about
all the bickering between the two Courts. She just sighed
and said in her weak voice, "The French are an odd lot." I
didn't know what to say back. It was a comment impossible to respond to. I wanted to say, "Then why am I being
sent there? Why must I learn all these stupid rules and
ways to play cards, walk, eat, and talk? Why are you sending me to this strange country where even my future husband seems not to care a whit for me and will not take the
time to write?"

And as all these very angry thoughts were running
through my head, Lulu said, "You know, my dear, they
want to take it off?"

I must not have been concentrating because I was
caught unawares. "What off?" I said. "What are you talking about?" Then Lulu's face turned dreadfully dark and
her eyes seemed to swim behind seas of tears. "You don't
know, Antonia? They didn't tell you?"

"Tell me what?" I asked. And I was suddenly filled with a terrible fear. Then she told me herself. Her leg is diseased. The Court surgeons want to cut it off. I gasped. If they cut it off, they feel, they can save her life. But she is frightened of the pain. They could give her only so much wine and strong spirits to make her senseless, but she would still feel the knives.

I could scarcely breathe as Lulu told me this story. This was so unimaginable to me. It was as if some terrible enemy grew within her own body. I always thought of enemies on the outside like Frederick of Prussia, The Monster. This thing that grows in dear Lulu's leg . . . Oh, I cannot bear to think of it any longer. What would I do? Would I ever be brave enough for the pain, and if I were could I bear the thought of being so mutilated?

February 23, 1770

Lulu died last night. They did not tell me until this morning. But I knew. A few minutes after midnight Schnitzel, who sleeps at the foot of my bed, began whining in his sleep. It woke me up. Everything was black. The last candles had guttered out, but one single shaft of moonlight pierced through the shutters and fell like a shard of ice on my floor. Something drew me to the window. I crawled out of my bed barefoot and ran across the cold wood. I looked out. The moon hung in the sky like a little scrap of fingernail. It was too little moon to cast so much light. Just a sliver, but in that moment I knew somehow that Lulu had passed from this earth. "Godspeed!" I whispered. And I could almost see her dancing through the night, her lovely legs all well and perhaps doing a Scottish reel right up into the stars. Oh yes, I shall imagine her prancing across the back of the Great Bear constellation, gliding up to the Swan and the Archer and all the starry figures of this winter night. If there is music in heaven, Lulu will find it and the angels will play better once she is there.

February 24, 1770

Mama has declared a two-week mourning period for Lulu. The period is to end right before the winter ball, but I am excused from going to it. For this I am grateful. Mama keeps saying we must carry on, even though I do know that she is quite sad, for she cared greatly for Lulu. But right or wrong I have a place in my heart for both these dear souls I have lost within the space of a month and I shall not simply carry on, but carry their memories with me until I am in my own grave.

March 1, 1770

It has been just one week since Lulu died, but Mama has already picked her replacement. Countess Krautzinger was waiting for me in my apartments when I returned from my riding lesson. I must say I think Mama could have given me a little warning. It is a shock to come back and find someone sitting in one's favorite chair by the fire directing one's chambermaid to "move quickly and fetch more tea and call for more kindling, and do find the claret bottle. What, there is no claret in the Archduchess's apartments?"

"I like not the claret." Those were my first words to the Countess. And the next words I had no need to say. They were silently spoken. How dare you come into my apartments and sit in my chair and order about my chambermaid and demand claret? Something amazing happened to me. I felt myself grow several inches in the space of seconds. The timbre of my voice changed. I know my eyes turned ice blue. I became in those fleeting seconds a Queen. And the Countess knew it as well. She immediately leapt from the chair and curtsied. "I am to be your new governess–Grand Mistress, My Lady," she whispered. And I replied, "It seems that I am not the only one who shall be learning." Brunhilda, my daytime chambermaid, nearly dropped the plate she was carrying. I quickly dismissed the Countess and then sat down and wrote in my finest hand a note to Mama.

My dear Majesty,
I was alarmed to find in my apartments this afternoon the Countess Krautzinger. She had made free with my quarters, sitting in my favorite chair and commanding my chambermaid in a manner that was most offensive. I regret that you did not see fit to inform me that the Countess would succeed my beloved Lulu, but I am even more disturbed that you would deem her to be an adequate Grand Mistress, considering her arrogance and complete lack of sensibility. I think that I shall not learn

much from her, and she stands to learn a great deal more from me.

Most respectfully, your daughter

Marie Antoinette

March 2, 1770

I received today the most astounding note from Mama. I paste it here in my diary.

> *Daughter, Bravo!*
> *You have excelled in the most important lesson I have put to you thus far; indeed, you have exceeded my expectations. Kraut is a fraud and a hypocrite. You have seen right through her and so quickly. Her arrogance is her shield for a weak character. But study her, for there will be many like her at Versailles. I have arranged for you to take card playing and gambling lessons from her. She will not*

tell you how she cheats but it will soon become apparent. You shall then be able to detect these behaviors in others and ban them from your gaming table. Do you not find her wart most interesting?

Most sincerely, your affectionate mother, Maria Theresa of Habsburg, Empress of the Holy Roman Empire, wife of your beloved late father, Emperor Francis of Lorraine

Postscript: Your hand has improved immensely and your spelling is flawless!

March 4, 1770

I do not know how I ever missed the wart on the Countess's nose. (I think of her now as Countess Sauer Kraut.) I must have been so upset by her behavior the first time I met with her that I completely lost sight of it. But there it is — large, red, and with a small hair growing out of it. It seems to have a life of its own, especially when we play cards. I think it twitches when she gets a good hand. It is most distracting, so I don't imagine I shall soon figure out how she cheats at cards. Of course she has been letting me win, I think. No real money is being played for, however. Perhaps I shall suggest we raise the stakes and then I'll try to concentrate on her tricks.

March 8, 1770

I suggested raising the stakes two days ago. The Countess continued to let me win until today, and today she won in a most large manner. Mama would be shocked if she knew how much money I lost. But I plan to continue, for I am sure I shall find out her tricky ways. I have told Elizabeth what Mama said and how I think the Countess now begins to cheat. Elizabeth has agreed to play, too, and to back me with more money if I need it. She is intrigued. Elizabeth has always enjoyed word games and puzzles. Thus she is fascinated and challenged by this.

March 12, 1770

Neither Elizabeth nor I can figure out how Sauer Kraut does it. She is devilishly clever. She lets us win just enough to keep us going so as not to be bored. Elizabeth has figured out the pattern. We are allowed to win a few hands at the start. Then she takes over in a streak of wins. Then if our interest flags, she lets us win again. Our interest really does not flag but Elizabeth and I decided to feign it so we could test to see if this indeed was the pattern. But then today Abbé de Vermond joined, and he put a gold piece on the table right off. You should have seen Sauer Kraut's eyes glitter! Needless to say, Countess Sauer Kraut broke her pattern and won the first hand.

March 17, 1770

My life these days seems to be spent either at the gaming table or the riding school. I must admit that I am getting sick of cards. Neither Elizabeth nor I can figure out how Sauer Kraut does it. When we sit at the gaming table it all seems lies and deceit. I have even begun to suspect that Abbé de Vermond might on occasion cheat when he plays with us. That perhaps is the worst part of this — one starts to suspect everyone. The air is so still, the apartments seem stuffy. The dust motes circulate in a slow minuet in stale shafts of sunlight. But in the riding school it is an entirely different world. The air is nippy. The chandeliers sparkle. The horses are so true.

March 18, 1770

I caught Sauer Kraut today almost ready to swat Schnitzy.
I was so mad. I wanted to scream at her, "So you not only
cheat at cards, you abuse animals." But I didn't say that,
for we want to learn her cheating tricks. However, I did
say that if I ever catch her lifting a hand again against
Schnitzy or any pet of the Court, I will go directly
to Mama. Everyone knows that Mama cannot abide
people who are cruel to animals. Sauer Kraut turned
white. Her face was frozen in fear.

March 20, 1770

Not feeling well today. My throat scratches. Courtiers from
Versailles are infesting the Hofburg. All the final plans are
being drawn up. Dates are set. My proxy marriage shall take
place on April 19. Two days before, on April 17, I must sign
what is called the Acts of Renunciation, whereby I promise
never to claim the throne of the Holy Roman Empire.

The French wear entirely too much perfume. One can
smell them coming kilometers away. And my brother
Joseph, who is certainly a very sensible fellow and not a

dandy at all, claims that one of their "blasted beauty marks" fell into a dish of soup he was being served. How this would have happened I know not. But not only do the women wear the little dark spots at the corner of their mouths or high on their cheeks but so do the men! I hope Louis Auguste does not wear one.

March 21, 1770

Have a high fever. Too sick to play cards or take my riding lessons.

March 22, 1770

Elizabeth came to visit me today and I thought I smelled some of that horrid French perfume on her, so I asked. "No" she replied. "But they all hover in the corridor outside your apartments." I became alarmed. "Am I to die? Is that why they hover?" I cried. She told me of course not, but that the French are often hysterical and consumed with fears about health and bodily functions. They talk, she tells me, unceasingly about their livers.

March 25, 1770

Elizabeth has figured out how Countess Sauer Kraut cheats. On her right hand she wears a large emerald ring. Apparently in the setting on the ring she has either a tiny pin, or perhaps it is just a rough point on the gold in which the emerald is set, but it allows her to prick the cards and thus mark them while she is playing. Elizabeth says she knows just how to mark them so that there is a very slight imperfection on the outside of the card in the design somewhere. Only a very sharp eye could see it, but Sauer Kraut has very sharp eyes!

March 26, 1770

Sicker today. The doctor has come twice and Mama has ordered away all the French courtiers who hover outside the door. I cannot write anymore because my head hurts so much.

March 31, 1770

Finally better, but Mama insists I stay in bed. For tomorrow the first of the official delegations of Vienna arrive to offer their formal congratulations to me. She wants me to look healthy and rested. I am only allowed up for my fittings for the gown in which I shall receive them. Herr Riding Master Francke sent an immense bouquet of lilies for me from Cabriole, my favorite horse.

April 1, 1770

Will write about the delegations later. Their arrival paled next to another, seemingly lesser, event that went unnoticed except by a few. We caught Sauer Kraut outright cheating. Oh, I should not claim the honor. It was not me, nor Elizabeth. It was Schnitzy! Schnitzy often sleeps under the gaming table as we play. Well, yesterday evening he was under the table and we heard him gnawing on something. I thought it was his favorite drumstick that the cook gave him last fall. But it wasn't. It was Sauer Kraut's shoe, which she had removed under the table. She often talks about her bunions and her sore feet. So she often excuses herself for removing her shoes. She bent over to retrieve the shoe and we heard a little yelp. Sauer Kraut rose up, her face not white but beet red, her eyes a livid greenish brown. Then we heard a terrible shriek and the table seemed to lurch. She had kicked Schnitzy. Schnitzy ran out from under the table with her shoe, and out of the shoe came two trump cards! The fiend! She has been hiding trumps in her shoes all these days. So not only does she mark the cards, but when her luck is really out she substitutes others! Is that not shameful?

She ran from the room! I now fear for Schnitzy's life.

April 2, 1770

The first of the delegations to arrive to offer me their congratulations consisted of twenty scholars from the University of Vienna. They addressed me in Latin. I understood hardly a word, but thankfully Abbé had prepared for me a short speech (very short, three sentences) in Latin and I was able to respond. Elizabeth tutored me in my response. She said I did very nicely. Postscript: Elizabeth and I told Mama about Sauer Kraut's deceptions at the gaming table. Mama just smiled and nodded. "She has served her purpose. I shall send her back to the *Frau-garten.*" That is what Mama calls the assembly rooms for the Ladies-in-Waiting. When I asked Mama why she didn't send her from the Court, Mama seemed appalled by my stupidity. "What? Where I cannot keep an eye on her? Never!"

April 3, 1770

Happiness!!! Oh, dearest diary, you shall never guess what happened today. At last I have heard from my dear future husband. The French ambassador Durfort arrived today and brought with him not one but <u>two</u> portraits of Louis Auguste — one for me and one for Mama. He is not un-comely, though his face seems a bit heavy, but still he has a pleasing countenance, just as Abbé de Vermond said. I much prefer this slightly heavy face to those of the pow-dered court dandies with their beauty spots. I have hung his portrait up in my apartments near the window by my desk. And now I confess that I have practiced speaking to it this evening. In the portrait his mouth is a straight, somewhat thin line, but I can tell that it easily could be brought to a most pleasing smile. So I try to think of amusing things to say. Riddles are always good. His Excellency the ambassador Durfort was most pleased with my reaction. He tells me that locks and locksmithing are of special interest to the Dauphin. I know absolutely nothing about such things. Elizabeth suggests that I send for the Court locksmith and have him show me some locks and explain them.

April 6, 1770

Locks are quite boring. No, not quite. Very. But for some they seem to be a passion. Herr Munchenmaas, the Imperial Court locksmith, was delighted to come to my apartments yesterday with an assortment of locks and explain to me their intricacies. Luckily, Elizabeth was here so she asked all the important questions. I was simply too bored to think of any. Here is what I have learned: The first locks were very primitive and invented in Egypt thousands of years ago. They were simple bolt locks. Then Herr Munchenmaas quoted the Old Testament prophet Isaiah. "I will place on his shoulders the key of the house of David." That allowed him to discourse for at least twenty minutes on the invention of keys, something called the falling-pin principle, tumblers, and all variety of mechanical pieces used for locks. Elizabeth has made a list of all the basic lock parts and has sketched them for me so that I might review them and thus educate myself for the Dauphin. I hope that the Dauphin has some other interest beyond locks that we might share.

April 10, 1770

Mama requires that I sleep in her apartments, indeed in her sleeping chamber in a bed next to hers. It is as if she feels there are not enough hours in the day before my departure for her to tell me all I need to know about marriage, and having babies, and treating servants and courtiers. She talks incessantly as our maids prepare us for sleep. It is interesting, but living so close to Mama I can see how she has aged so much in the past two years. When her maid undresses her, I can see how her skin sags, especially around her neck, how despite her plumpness there is a frailty to her body. Without her switches and braids, her own hair barely covers her head, and her skull appears as small and fragile as a porcelain bowl. Mama is fifty-four. This is a great age, I know. But there are some at fifty-four who appear much younger, but then again they are not Empresses of the Holy Roman Empire. And they do not have to deal with monsters like Frederick of Prussia. I vow that I shall listen carefully to Mama and take her lessons to heart. I do not want her to have to worry about me.

April 12, 1770

Barely a minute to write. I have been subjected to hours upon hours of fittings for my new French wardrobe. My journey to France begins in less than two weeks!! My marriage by proxy takes place within a week.

April 13, 1770

Last night as Mama and I knelt in prayer before bed, I noticed a tremor in her hands. Once more I was struck by how old Mama has become. I hope I shall fare better. I just would hate to have my skin creased and slack like hers is. And the parts that are smooth are mottled and gray. Fifty-four is an unimaginable age to me. She has had so many cares, however. I pray that as the Dauphine and future

Queen of France my way shall be somewhat easier. The French have a large capacity for gaiety and diversion. This should help me. And of course the Court is so rich. Mama worries about budgets and money matters so much. I don't really think one needs to worry quite that much.

April 14, 1770

Tomorrow the French ambassador Durfort is to arrive with the Royal entourage that is to accompany me. I have been in meetings with Mama and Prince Kaunitz and our ambassador to the French Court, Count Mercy, all day. There are over one thousand people in the entourage. I found these meetings very hard, for I have learned for the first time how few of my own things I shall be able to take with me to France. Not one of my chambermaids may travel with me beyond the French border. None of the horse grooms that I have come to know over the years. There will hardly be a familiar face, save that of Abbé de Vermond. At the border, near the city of Strasbourg at the abbey of Schüttern, I shall meet my new Ladies-in-Waiting and servants. Not only am I not allowed to take along the dear people who have served me so well as long as

I can remember, but none of my personal possessions, none of my clothes. I began to cry, much to Mama's dismay. I begged to take Schnitzy. They say they shall think upon it.

April 15, 1770

We stood for three hours on the balcony and watched the procession enter the grand courtyard of the Hofburg. In all there were forty-eight coaches drawn by six horses each, including the immense gilt Berlins specially ordered for me by Louis XV. I cannot wait to see the inside of the Berlins. I understand they are plushly lined with blue velvet, have small crystal chandeliers and a table for a complete tea service! There were over one hundred equerries, or horse officers, just for the coaches.

April 16, 1770

The official reception to welcome Ambassador Durfort as representative of Louis XV was tonight. There were two performances, including a ballet especially choreographed by Noverre. I could not help but remember our performances of this summer and our ballet with Titi at

Schönbrunn. For this event I had to spend six hours with four hairdressers. I shall not sleep well tonight at all for I must give up my pillow for the wooden block to preserve my hairdo. However, Liesel, my chambermaid, promises to put a thick wadding of cotton on the neck rest.

April 17, 1770

Today at noon sharp in the Hofburg's high conference room in the presence of Mama and my brother Joseph, their ministers and councillors, I signed the Acts of Renunciation of all my rights as a descendant of the Habsburg dynasty. This means that neither I nor any of my future children can ever claim any rights to the throne. Joseph, who rules alongside Mama as Emperor, retains all such rights for himself and his children. I had to swear an oath on a Bible. It felt odd. I have always lived in Austria, been Austrian, and now with this I remove myself from Austria. It is a mental removal. It is to serve as a signal to my mind that I can no longer claim what I was born to. In four days there will be a physical removal as I climb into one of the two Berlins to be driven away from the country of my birth.

P.S. Elizabeth came bursting into my apartment just a few minutes ago with the wonderful news that I am to be allowed to take Schnitzy with me to France. I was seized with happiness, but as I bent to scoop up Schnitzy, I was suddenly struck by the cold truth: how much I would rather take Elizabeth, and when shall I ever see her again? As I rose up, I could spy in Elizabeth's eyes, even through her veil, a mirror image of the same thoughts. We rushed to each other and embraced with Schnitzy squashed between us. Schnitzy was yipping and we were crying, our cheeks so wet and salty with tears that Schnitzy began licking our faces and then we started laughing. Oh, I am so mixed up. I laugh. I cry. I cannot sort out my feelings. And in two days I shall be married by proxy.

April 18, 1770

Ferdinand and I practiced today the proxy ceremony for marriage. We could not help but giggle. It is hard not to, for after all we have been brother and sister all these years, racing our ponies, playing games and tricks. To have him now as a substitute groom and me a bride seems ridiculous. Is it just another game? I remember so well when

Ferdinand slipped a small frog under the silver dome of my favorite dessert, Vienna torte. Instead of fluffy white whipped cream there was this tiny quivering green frog. We all nearly hurt ourselves laughing.

Now when Ferdinand and I kneel together in the church of the Augustins as we did this afternoon in practice, all I can think of is that little green frog and I just start laughing. At first I pretended I was coughing but I could not keep up that deceit for long. Ferdinand knew exactly what I was thinking, and he started making funny faces and then choking because he was convulsed with giggles, too. Oh my goodness, it was agony. Count Mercy spoke severely to us. We finally did it right, without laughing.

April 19, 1770

I'm married and I feel not one speck different than I did before. Ferdinand and I did perfectly in the ceremony. It was hard to believe I could ever have dreamed I might laugh, for it was so solemn. I walked through an honor guard of two hundred Royal grenadiers to the church of the Augustins which adjoins the palace. My dress was of silver and with a train of more than thirty feet. Mama's old and very dear friend the Countess of Trautmannsdorff carried my train. I understand that Countess Sauer Kraut was very upset, for she had expected to carry my train. But I have always loved "Trautie," as Mama calls her, and she will be in my entourage to the border. When Ferdinand slid the ring onto my finger, I tried to picture Louis Auguste but for some reason I simply could not capture his face, although his portrait has been on my wall now for several days.

This evening I wrote a letter to my new father-in-law, King Louis XV, and my husband, the Dauphin, to inform them that my marriage has been celebrated. I signed the letter Antonia. Mama did not object, which surprised me. But this is the last time I shall ever sign my name thusly. Henceforth it shall be only Marie Antoinette. I am told that the name Antonia does not exist in France. After a day of rest I leave. Our procession of carriages and equerries and attendants is said to stretch almost two miles in length.

It is cold and rainy and this castle seems to me inadequately heated. I have asked Trautie how we are expected to dress for the Prince's banquet if it is this cold in the banquet hall. Thank goodness Trautie is so no-nonsense. She says that she plans to wear flannel unders and I can do as I please. This is what I love about Trautie. She never tells one what to do. She leads by firm example.

Our first night was spent at Melk in an abbey. My brother Joseph accompanied us this far. There was an opera performed by the monastery's singing students. They were terrible. It just shows that what Mama says is true — if one removes to anywhere outside of the circumference of Vienna, the music worsens. The farther one travels away from Vienna, the worse the music gets.

The coach we ride in — the Berlin — is as wonderful as described. In fact, Trautie said that tonight we might be more comfortable in the Berlin than in this cold stone room of the castle. I plan to have Schnitzy sleep under the covers with me. I certainly don't want him catching cold.

He is all I can carry with me over the border from my old life.

April 25, 1770
Alt Ettingen, Bavaria

It is amazing, the sameness of the days. I feel inadequate to the journey, for I am easily bored when I look out the window of the Berlin as we pass through the countryside or through the small villages where people come out to wave and cheer. Mama would be so enthralled, for this is her kingdom and there is not a corner of it that does not interest her. Indeed, we are passing through all of the little states that form the Empire. We are now in that part called the Holy Roman German Empire, but it is still under the rule of Mama and Joseph.

We are coming close to Munich now and there are many festivities planned for my stay. The Elector of Bavaria lives there and is one of the richest men in all of Europe. His shooting lodge at Amalienburg and his gardens are supposed to be extraordinary. We sent news back to Vienna by courier. I have prepared letters for Mama and for Elizabeth and Ferdinand. It was very difficult for me to write Elizabeth. I realized that I have not talked much of the good-byes I had to bid when we left. It is simply too painful, but to say good-bye to Elizabeth was the worst. I feel a cold coming on.

April 28, 1770
Augsburg, Germany

We all have terrible colds. No wonder! It has done nothing but rain since we left Vienna. My aunt Charlotte, my father's sister, whom I have never met, shall receive me tomorrow at the abbey of Günsburg, where she is the Abbess.

April 29, 1770

I am so happy to be here and because we all have colds we are to stay a few days longer. My aunt Charlotte is the most wonderful woman. I can so easily see the traces of my dear father's face in hers. She is the perfect blend of quiet jolliness and tenderness. I wish I could stay here forever. She runs the abbey with a gentle efficiency and it is a lovely abbey, for Augsburg is one of the richest cities in the Empire.

May 1, 1770

My days with Aunt Charlotte seemed charmed. She has taught me a new embroidery stitch, and we sit in her cozy quarters sipping tea and I tell her about all of her nieces and nephews. She laughed so hard when I told her about how Ferdinand put the frog in my dessert. Then she told me many funny stories about father and when they were growing up in Lorraine. She promises tomorrow, if my cold is much better, to take me to the edge of the meadow beyond the abbey, near the forest where the wild asparagus grows. She says it is the most delicious thing that God ever let grow on earth. I can't wait. But I must admit that I fear it could be spoiled if Count Mercy or Ambassador Durfort insist that the usual entourage accompany us.

May 2, 1770

Oh, it is late, but I must write about Aunt Charlotte's and my wonderful day. It began with quiet words between

Aunt Charlotte and yes, as you might guess, Count Mercy and Durfort. No, she would not hear of a large entourage. She would only allow two equerries to accompany us and Trautie. And you will not believe this, but she got her way. She told them simply and directly that the meadow was a place of peace and beauty, where indeed if one came to it in a quiet manner, the animals would not be disturbed, for there are lovely birds, and little squirrels and field mice, and sometimes deer. She told them that she wanted me to see all these things for they were simple, good things blessed by God, and I would have precious little occasion to enjoy the natural world once I got to the Court. She would not allow fifty grenadiers and equerries with their horses and clanging swords to come tromping across God's meadow.

So we went. Just the five of us with two picnic hampers and small spades to dig the asparagus. And I saw everything — the deer, the titmouse, a meadowlark, a red-tailed hawk flying over the field, and yes, a doe at the forest's edge with her mother.

We dug the asparagus, and tonight Aunt Charlotte cooked it for me herself with butter and melted cheese. I ate a whole plateful and drank half the brown jug of sweet milk. Then I had two slices of the thick coarse-grain bread that Aunt and the nuns make fresh every day.

I said to Trautie tonight that I now understand why a woman would choose to be religious and seek a cloistered life. You submit to just one person, Jesus Christ. He is your husband, your protector. To be a true bride of Christ is to be more powerful than to be Queen of an Empire.

May 3, 1770

We are all unfortunately getting over our colds. I fear we shall be leaving within two days. I shall be so sad.

May 4, 1770

We leave tomorrow. I tried to make Aunt Charlotte promise me that she would visit at Versailles. And she began to say, "Oh no, my dear, Versailles . . . ." But then she realized what she was saying and very quietly said to me, "One does not have to be near someone to know where they are or how they feel. It is possible, dear Antonia, to commune over great distances." I think what she says might be true, but what she did not say is possibly true as well, and that was what she began to say but never finished: "Versailles is no place to be for one who dwells within the spirit of Christ."

This leave-taking tomorrow might be the hardest good-bye.

May 5, 1770
Riedlingen, Duchy of Württemberg, Germany

We are at the town of Riedlingen, just beside the Danube. The river smells horribly. I try only to remember the taste of the asparagus that Aunt Charlotte cooked for me.

May 6, 1770
Schüttern Abbey near Strasbourg

We arrived tonight at the abbey, our last resting stop before the border between the Empire and France. We are all very tired. In a few minutes I shall meet my new Lady-in-Waiting, the first Lady of Honor or the Dame d'Honneur, and her husband, the Count and the Countess de Noailles. The Count is another high-ranking ambassador of the French king.

P.S.: It is late. I have met the Count and the Countess. I like them not. They are full of self-importance. The Count barely acknowledged me. He was consumed with some wording in a document that he considered insulting to the Court at Versailles. There was a bit of a to-do between him and Count Mercy over this. I was completely ignored. I feel that the Count's behavior toward me was more of an insult than anything written on a paper. I was, after all, right there in the room. The Countess seemed more concerned with the Count than with me. And so tomorrow I must say good-bye to the good, sensible Trautie and have in her stead this woman who seems to sneer constantly.

May 7, 1770

I could not sleep. I write now in the dimmest light of dawn. Today is the ceremony of the *remise,* or the delivery. The delivery of me. It is to take place on neither Austrian nor French soil, but as close as one can come to neutral ground, an island in the middle of the Rhine River. There is a building that has been especially constructed for the ceremony. I am, however, still not quite sure what the ceremony is. People have been vague about it. I shall write more later. In a few hours I am to put on my gown for the ceremony along with my Austrian jewels, but then immediately following I am to change my clothing again.

Later: Strasbourg

It is now near midnight. I cannot sleep although I am so tired. There are to be two days of festivities. I must smile. I must look gracious. I must listen attentively, but now, dear diary, please listen to me, for I may cry, I may grimace, and I must pour out my heart. Today's ceremony was the hardest thing I have ever done. The *remise* was supposed to be a ceremony of state. I cannot think of it as anything but a funeral — my own! I had the odd sensation of standing outside my own body and watching as people disposed of it as they willed.

At midday I was taken by boat to the Isle des Epis in the middle of two branches of the Rhine near the gates of the city of Strasbourg. I walked then through two rows of soldiers and a crowd of a thousand to a makeshift building. I entered one door which was on the Austrian side of the border. There was a large drawing room hung with tapestries, and I was to sit down in a chair on a platform under a canopy. There were long speeches and much passing of documents. Outside it began to pour and perhaps because this building had been so quickly constructed there were some leaks, but in many places streams of water poured in. I saw the Countess de Noailles edging away from a puddle. Everyone ignored the rain, for their eyes were fastened on me. I, however, did not. I studied with ferocity the plinking of the drops straight in front of my chair. In this way I could hold my head erect and appear calm, as hundreds of eyes seemed to feast on me. The raindrops were my only diversion, my only comfort. So absorbed had I been with the raindrops that I failed to notice that most of the people in the room had left, including the entire Austrian delegation, and that I was alone in the midst of foreigners. Count Mercy gone. Trautie gone. Brunhilda gone. My groomsmen and equerries gone. And standing before me were the Count and Countess de Noailles, their sharp faces pallid, with a slightly greenish tinge. The Count's beauty mark had slid to an unfashionable position near his ear.

I was then directed to a room off the main hall. There I was at first delighted to see my old servants Brunhilda and Trautie and several other chambermaids. But I was shocked when they told me that the orders were for me to take off every stitch of clothing, including my pantaloons and stockings and chemise, and to leave these Austrian clothes behind. I was then to walk through a door to another room completely naked! Trautie assured me that there would be no men, only women, to meet me, and that when I passed through this portal to the other room I would have crossed some invisible frontier and entered France. I would then be dressed entirely in French clothing.

So they began to remove my dress, my rings, my shoes. Not a buckle or lace hanky could travel across. Although I was as naked as the day I was born, I felt death in the air. I was a body being prepared for the burial. I was to curtsy to the Countess de Noailles, who stood holding a robe of golden drapery, but I cannot curtsy naked. Instead I rushed at her and snatched the robe with such shocking speed that there was a gasp from all the other Ladies-in-Waiting. The Countess hissed at me that only she as the Lady of Honor was to cloak me in the robe and that I was to curtsy to acknowledge her position as the highest ranking of the ladies in Royal service. "That is the etiquette." I did not reply. I merely wrapped myself tighter in the robe. I wanted to scream at her, "Corpses don't curtsy, you idiot!" but I did not.

May 9, 1770
Castle of Saverne outside of Strasbourg

I am somewhat recovered from my ordeal on the Isle des Epis. However, I do not know if I shall ever adjust to the Countess de Noailles. The only thing that makes her any better than old Sauer Kraut is that so far I do not think she cheats at cards. We played a few hands last night. Little did I realize when she hissed at my refusal to curtsy, "That is the etiquette!" that indeed she would find occasion to say it at least forty times in the following two days. It is her favorite phrase. I think I shall call her Madame Etiquette.

Every night there have been festivities and performances in my honor. There was a ball, and this morning a High Mass was celebrated by the Bishop of Strasbourg. Then yesterday there was a wonderful procession through the streets with jugglers, clowns, and acrobats. I was introduced by the Cardinal to a woman said to be one hundred and five years old. She was as tiny as a child and as wrinkled as a raisin, but her eyes were clear and her voice crisp. She stepped right up to me and said, "Princess, I pray to heaven that you may live as long as myself and as free of sickness." I replied that I wish it may be so if it is for the well-being of France. Even the Countess de Noailles nodded and gave a smile at my reply.

Every time I say anything proper, the Countess seems surprised, and perhaps especially with my excellent French. I cannot believe that she does not know that French is, after all, the language of the Court of the Habsburgs. It is the writing of French that gives me a problem, and the writing of German, for that matter. But look how I have improved. Look how interesting my sentences have become since I started. As my writing has improved and my sentences have become more interesting, I do believe that my thinking has become more interesting. I think about people and actions in a new way now — and most of all, I reflect on my feelings deeply, sometimes too deeply.

Now we are on our way to Paris and are staying at the palace of the Bishop of Strasbourg in Saverne. It is quite grand.

May 11, 1770

We are expected to arrive at La Compiègne within the next three days. This is the favorite hunting forest of the King and the Dauphin. They will be there. I am so nervous! I cannot concentrate any longer on all the throngs of people and the festive banners that greet us in every town we pass through. The Countess de Noailles talks constantly — etiquette, what else. She is an uninterrupted stream of instructions on what I am to do when we get to La Compiègne. How I am to descend from the carriage. How I shall curtsy. How I shall first greet my grandfather-in-law, the King. How I shall fold my hands when we sit all of us together in the carriage. How I must receive the respects of the other Ladies-in-Waiting who shall meet us there. Countess de Noailles has me practice the curtsy to the King at least five times before I retire every night. It is complicated, but my dance master Noverre prepared me well. I think she is surprised.

It is not a simple curtsy. It takes place in four parts. First one must sink partway down. One's left leg is partially extended behind. Then for the next part it is fully extended, and with one's arms one must sweep one's gown back. One must hold this position for a full fifteen seconds counting one, one thousand, two, one thousand, and so on. Then one rises in the same manner. I do it well but the Countess always finds something wrong. She is indeed a tiresome lady. I cannot imagine living to one hundred and five years with her as my Lady of Honor.

May 14, 1770
Pont de Berne, near La Compiègne

I am numb. It is all I can do to push this pen across the paper. I have met at last the Dauphin of France, my husband Louis Auguste. He is <u>horrible!</u> I don't know where to begin.

When we arrived at Pont de Berne the sun was shining brightly. The world seemed to sparkle. I did exactly as the Countess de Noailles instructed me. I walked between my Knight of Honor and first equerry toward the King. The King is one of the most handsome men I have ever seen. Surely, I thought, his grandson will be handsome. My curtsy was perfect and I did not even have to hold it the required fifteen seconds, for soon the King himself had bent over and put his kind hand under my chin and raised me up, then kissed me on both cheeks, and spoke most charmingly to me. I did not yet spy the Dauphin. Then the King called in a somewhat sharp tone, "Louis! Louis! Come, fellow, come up and meet your lovely little bride."

Imagine my horror when this large awkward boy came shambling up, his eyes not on me but on the ground. I saw the consternation in the King's face, and I also saw him give the Dauphin a poke in the ribs. Louis Auguste came forward. I thought I might faint. I was absolutely repelled. He looks nothing like his picture. He is fat and oafish. His skin has pimples. His eyes are dim and squinty. He smells, but worst of all he is not very nice. I feel like such a fool, such a fool. I had such high hopes. To think that I was worried what he might think of me, that I would not be pretty enough! I had even entertained the notion that the Dauphin might be the most handsome young man on earth, or a god from Mount Olympus! Phuff! What a fool I have been!

Here I have spent over a year of my life being educated, learning etiquette and proper manners for this Court, and this ugly oaf can hardly speak. In the carriage I was seated between him and his grandfather. The Dauphin said not

149

one single word. He did nothing but look at his feet and then pick his fingernails, which were dirty!

We have just been taken to the chateau of Compiègne and, thank goodness, shown to separate rooms.

The King's Master of Ceremonies has just left after having been led in by the Countess. He presented me with twelve wedding rings to try on to see which fit best. None did, really. I settled for the loosest.

May 15, 1770,
Muette Castle, near Versailles

The roadways were so choked with people to see me that the carriages crawled like snails. We were forced to stop this evening at this castle, La Muette, a few miles from Versailles. We had what the French Royal Family, the Bourbons, consider a "small family supper." There were only thirty-five of us. I have met for the first time the Dauphin's brothers, my brothers-in-law. They are both so handsome! What happened to Louis Auguste? However, one of the brothers, the Count of Provence, who is just my age, is quite conceited and terribly delighted with himself. The other brother, the Count Artois, who is a year younger than me, is completely charming. A bit shy, but ready to talk about books and horses and games. Both of them are so much better than their brother. It is not fair! Why am I set to marry the fat one with pimples, who never talks and has dirty nails?

I noticed as we sat at the table that at the far end there was a somewhat coarse-looking young woman. Take away her powdered hair and her many jewels, and she would have had the look of the street about her. I inquired of the Count Artois who she was. He looked uncomfortable when I asked, but his brother chimed in, "Oh, the Countess du Barry!" He sneered and the people near us at the table fell silent. I think it is perfectly terrible that the King brought his mistress to this "family dinner." I feel gravely offended but the solace is that I am not the only one. Everyone at the table was shocked. The Countess de Noailles fumed later in my apartments. This is the first thing upon which she and I have agreed. It is odd but suddenly the King lost all his handsomeness for me. He seemed very common. I saw flaws. His chin sags a bit too much. His right eye droops and his mouth is much too fleshy.

Later: I just went into my bedchamber. I found placed directly on the bed a leather casket about one foot wide and equally long and perhaps eight inches high. I undid the clasp and opened the lid. My eyes were dazzled. Inside were rubies, emeralds, and diamonds — necklaces, bracelets, and earrings. A note said simply, "These are the jewels of France worn by all her Queens. They are now yours. Affectionately, your grandfather-in-law, King Louis XV."

Tomorrow our party drives on to Versailles. Tomorrow is the wedding, the real wedding, where Louis and I shall together walk down a corridor to the famous Hall of Mirrors at Versailles and on to the chapel. The weather does not look promising. But what do I care if it rains on my wedding day? It would be an outrage for the sun to shine. I feel no happiness at all. Just dread and fear.

May 17, 1770
Versailles

I am married.

When I was married by proxy a month ago with Ferdinand standing in for the Dauphin, I said that I felt no different. I feel no different today, but that does not mean I do not feel something. Louis and I walked down the long corridor of mirrors. The rain had finally stopped for a period, and sunlight pierced the highest windows, making the brocades and jewels of the over two thousand people who lined the room shimmer. But no one indeed glittered more fiercely than I did. With the four thousand diamonds that studded my dress to reflect the sun's rays, I was caught in a firestorm of spangled light. We entered the chapel of Louis XIV, the King's great-grandfather. It is a dazzling place of white marble and gold. The organ pipes soar many feet into the air from the gallery above, and scenes from the life of Christ are painted and sculpted throughout the chapel. But what drew my eyes was a beautiful gold relief of King David on the screen of the organ. He seems frozen in time, without movement, yet plucking the strings of his harp. Perhaps his music is heard only by God, but perhaps it is like Mama has said — the farther one travels from Vienna, the more the music diminishes — perhaps there is no real music in France.

The thought struck me as so sad that I felt my eyes well up with tears and then I felt my hand being squeezed. It was indeed Louis Auguste, who was looking at me with a mixture of sadness and fear in his own eyes. In that moment my heart went out to him. *He is as scared as I am,* I thought, and I realized that although I might not love Louis Auguste, I can be his friend. We shall get through this together some-how. I must go now, for it is time for the presentation of my household. This is when I meet all of my Ladies-in-Waiting and the servants who shall attend me.

Later: At the Hofburg I was attended to mainly by six people. Three chambermaids, my Grand Mistress, my music teacher, and sometimes a tutor and Father Confessor. Here I have nearly two hundred. There are nine ushers alone to present people to me, six equerries for when I go out on horseback or in a carriage, two doctors, four surgeons, a clock maker, a wig maker, cooks, butlers, wine bearers, attendants to the bath, fourteen ladies just to wait on me in my chambers dealing with linen and cloth-ing, and then twelve aristocratic Ladies-in-Waiting to be available for card playing, chatting, and walking! No won-der my apartments are so large! How else would everyone fit in?

May 18, 1770

I cannot believe this. Today I took my first bath since ar-riving here and I found in my salon of the bath no fewer than eight women with the Countess of Noailles standing by the bath bewigged, in her jewels and full hooped gown. I was expected to undress and get into the bath and then, according to etiquette, the Countess would hand soap and toweling to the tirewoman, who is the lady in charge of my gowns and petticoats. Then she would hand that to the Lady of the Bedchamber, who would hand it to *la femme du bain*, the Lady of the Bath, and she would bathe me! I have bathed myself since I was six. My chambermaids would draw the water and they all had charming rhymes to help me remember to wash behind my ears, but what do these women take me for, a complete idiot? I am expected once again to strip naked in front of total strangers. I thank you <u>not!</u> Well, Madame Etiquette turned her usual shade of green. "In our country," she began. I knew what she would say next and I would have none of it. I immediately demanded a flannel gown. Behind a screen I undressed myself and reappeared in a nightrail of flannel. I stepped into the tub. This was my compromise. If they insist on being there and bathing me, I shall not show one speck of flesh. The toweling and sponges with the soap work fairly well, but I managed finally to wrestle one from the Lady of the Bath and scrub underneath the rail.

May 22, 1770

How shall I ever accustom myself to the stink of Versailles? It is unimaginable. They have not enough privies for all the people who mill about. There are upwards of six thousand people who have business here every day. There are five times as many nobles here as were ever at the Hofburg and not one-third the privies. People relieve themselves in the corners of the corridors. Although there is a rule and regulation for almost every aspect of life, from playing cards to eating and getting dressed and curtsying, there seems to be none about urinating. It makes all their etiquette seem even sillier.

And that is another thing. I believe I am growing thin, for I find it very difficult to eat with an audience of a thousand people. Yes! Can you believe that is what they do here? Nearly every day we must dine in public. On some occasions each branch of our family dines separately but at the same time in connecting salons. The ushers allow anyone in to view us who is appropriately dressed. But these viewers might tire of watching Louis and me sip our bouillon and then decide to run to the next salon, where the King and Madame du Barry have started their dessert. And then when it is what is called a Grand Couvert, we all dine together in a great hall and there is a gallery that overlooks our long table. Hundreds of people view us from above. This is enough to take one's appetite away, or at least mine. Not the Dauphin. He plows through mountains of food. At the end of some courses he belches loudly and everyone smiles. I am surprised they do not applaud! Such are the mysteries of etiquette at Versailles.

May 24, 1770

I wonder if I shall ever have another private moment in my life. There are always people to witness practically every moment of my day. This is the great pastime for noble men and women of Versailles. Watch the Dauphine take her morning coffee. Watch the Dauphine have her hair dressed and rouge put on. Rouge is required here. I never wore it in Vienna. I have not put on a stocking or buckled a shoe myself since I have arrived. Mama would not approve. But it is The Etiquette!

One reaches my apartments by what is called the Queen's staircase. The first room one enters is the chamber of my guards.

The next room is the antechamber. It is vast. This is where many nobles gather throughout the day. Madame Etiquette delights in appearing in the doorway here and announcing which noblemen and noblewomen may come in at what times to view me, or possibly play cards. The next room is my official drawing room. Here I spend a good deal of my day always surrounded by my Ladies-in-Waiting.

Next comes my bedchamber. Now, this is my favorite room and if I could only spend more time in it alone with none of my *femmes de chambre*, bedchamber women, and others like Madame Etiquette, it would be perfect. The best part has to be the ceiling. It was painted by the famous French painter Boucher and is a lovely gilded sky. A low gold railing separates the bed from the rest of the room. It is in this bed that all the Royal children have been born, and since these births are always witnessed by the public, and the noblemen and -women are brought directly into the bedchamber, the railing serves to keep the space around the bed clear for the doctor and the midwives. There is still a crack in the railing from when the crowd pressed for the last Royal birth, which was that of the Dauphin's youngest sister, Elisabeth, who is just six. His other younger sister, Clothilde, is eleven.

I wish they would let Clothilde and Elisabeth come to my apartments more to play. I could show them all the games that Titi and I played. I try not to think about Titi. It makes me so sad. I try not to think about many things these days. It is hard not to think of something, because just the act of not thinking about it makes you think about it! And of course, there is no privacy to have any real thoughts in anyhow. So what does it matter?

May 26, 1770

I have been invited to the apartments of the King's daughters and the Dauphin's aunts. They are three maiden sisters. None of them has ever married. Their names are Adelaide, Victoire, and Sophie. They are not particularly attractive. Indeed, Sophie is truly ugly and somewhat cold. Adelaide is very outgoing, and poor Victoire seems frightened of everything. But they welcomed me warmly into their apartments and invited me to play cards. In the course of the evening they managed to make many cutting remarks about Madame du Barry. They refuse to call her the Countess, although she has been given that title. But now that I have found out that the King himself has the most loathsome nicknames for his daughters — Rag, Piggy, and Snip — I think that they are perfectly justified in calling her Madame du Barry instead of Countess. And she was a simple mademoiselle before she met the King. They told me <u>all</u> about her. She did come from the streets of Paris, and the King married her off to a Count so she could be part of his Court. Her husband does not care because apparently he benefits greatly from having a wife who is a favorite of the King. This I guess is what Versailles calls etiquette. Lulu never taught me any of these lessons.

June 1, 1770

I have played cards several times this week with the Aunts. I am not sure whether they seek me out for my card-playing ability or the opportunity to gossip about Madame du Barry. I am a good listener, which is valued by them, I think. But while I am listening I am also watching. There is a lovely young woman who attends them in their apartments. I noticed her the first time. Last night she joined our card table. She is full of wit and charm. Her name is Madame Campan and she serves as Reader for the sisters, mostly for Princess Victoire. This is an official position and she reads to them every day at length — poetry, novels, and the like. When she came here she was unmarried, but now she has married. I doubt if she is more than twenty years old. But I like her a lot. I wish she could be my Reader. Indeed, I wish she could be my Lady of Honor instead of Madame Etiquette.

June 3, 1770

The days fall into a pattern. I have written Mama exactly what I do. I rise at nine or ten. The wardrobe woman brings me a book with drawings of all my dresses, and I select the ones I shall be wearing that day. The undertirewoman follows with a basket called *pret du jour* containing the linens I shall be wearing — chemises, stockings, and handkerchiefs. My Lady of Honor, Countess de Noailles, pours water on my hands and puts on my body linen, my undergarments. Only she is allowed to do this.

After dressing in the presence of at least eight Ladies of

My Chamber, who each hand me various garments according to etiquette and who may touch what, I say my morning prayers. I pray always first for Mama and Elizabeth and Father and then for Titi and Lulu. I pray finally for Louis Auguste and the King, and Louis's aunts. Then I have breakfast and I usually visit the Aunts. The King is often there, teasing them mercilessly.

At eleven o'clock I must go back to my apartments for the Grand Toilette, where a hairdresser awaits to dress my hair for the more public part of the day. This takes at least two hours. Everyone is then called into my chamber while an undertirewoman applies my rouge. Ladies and men are present. This is considered part of the entertainment in the French Court. If you are a noble and fix it with the right people, you are allowed to watch a Princess put on rouge and wash her hands. The men then leave, but the women remain and I change from my morning gown to my afternoon frock. I dress in front of them all!

Next is Mass with the Dauphin and the King. Then luncheon. Then I go to Louis Auguste's apartments. Usually it is for no more than an hour. I try to engage him in conversation. I even tried yesterday to say something about locks. But he rarely speaks to me. I won't give up. I am stronger than he is. I know this. I shall make him my friend.

Then another afternoon visit to my Aunts. The Abbé comes at four to see how I am doing. I lie and say excellent. The singing and harpsichord teacher comes at five for my lesson. Then I rest or take a walk. I am not allowed to walk with fewer than ten Ladies-in-Waiting. At seven I go back to the Aunts to play cards until nine and then we go to the public dining. If the King is dining alone with du Barry (I no longer call her even Madame. I really can't bear her. She is so smug and flaunts her bosom in a most unseemly manner), we must wait for him until eleven to say our official goodnights.

June 5, 1770

I have induced one of the underchambermaids to bring her little four-year-old daughter into the apartments occasionally. And the Dauphin asked if his first valet would permit his son who is five to come visit. I love children. They are so lively, these two. I do wish that I had Titi's mechanical theater here. It would be so much fun. They enjoy Schnitzy very much and have taken to teaching him tricks. We sometimes go out into the gardens. I am shocked that the gardens are not very well kept here. They are not nearly as nice as those at Schönbrunn, and it would be impossible to wade in the fountains, for many have broken basins and are filled with old muddy rainwater.

June 6, 1770

Madame Campan came to visit me today. How I do like that woman! I asked her if she would read to me and she said yes. I think this is a grand idea, for Mama's instructions before I left, and when she writes to me, are to keep reading books of worth and great merit. I am, however, to read nothing that the Abbé would not approve.

June 8, 1770

I see Madame du Barry almost every evening. Several times a week there are musical entertainments or large card parties. I avoid her. Etiquette does not permit her to talk to me until I have spoken to her. So far I have managed not to and I plan to keep it this way. This is the one time that the Countess de Noailles has not reprimanded me. If it had been anyone except for du Barry, she would have scolded me for not uttering at least the minimal greeting that allows one to speak: "And does this weather agree with you?" if it is not sunny or rainy. And if it is rainy or sunny, "What think you of this weather?"

June 18, 1770

Bless Madame Campan. She showed me something most unusual and it is indeed a treasure. My apartments have a secret staircase that leads to other rooms! Rooms that can be used by me and me alone. In this way I might seek some privacy. These were rooms designed and used by Queen Maria Leczinska. But everyone seems to have forgotten to tell me about them. Madame Campan says they have forgotten "on purpose," for they want me to be continually in public view. Well, enough of that. They are rather old and musty now, but if they could be cleaned, freshened, and painted, and with new furnishings — oh, how delightful they could be. They say that Versailles is a palace of over one thousand windows, and I feel as if they all look upon me, but with these private rooms, I could have some time away from the terrible glare of the Court. I plan to talk to Louis Auguste about it immediately.

June 20, 1770

I absolutely hate the Dauphin's tutor, the Duc de la Vauguyon. He is haughty and secretive and I am sure that when I send my requests to meet with the Dauphin at times other than meals and those prescribed, he does not deliver my messages. He is very close to du Barry. Between the two of them they have a network of spies. I am sure my messages are intercepted and read. I have been trying to see the Dauphin for the last three days about the cleaning of the private suite of rooms, but he is never available. It is considered terrible etiquette to bring up such a matter at a public function such as a meal or at card playing in one of the grand salons, and Louis Auguste has not been to his aunts' apartments these past several days. I do not know what to do.

June 21, 1770

Bless Madame Campan. She is a woman of wit and daring. She hates the Duc de la Vauguyon as much as I do. She has come up with a brilliant suggestion. Three mornings a week we are required to attend the Grand Levée, or the rising of the King. Included in this gathering are all the members of the Royal family, the King's physician and surgeon, the ministers of the cabinet, the Grand Chamberlain, the Grand Master and the Master of the Robes, and the First Valet of the Robes. The King has actually been up for at least an hour to use the *chaise percée,* the commode in the privy, but even there he is not alone. The Royal Physician is with him as well as the Privy Chamberlain. But by the time we arrive, he is back in bed with the curtains drawn. The First Gentleman of the Bedchamber goes up to the bed and draws the curtains. Everyone applauds when they see the King to show that we are happy that he did not die during the night. Then various valets come to the bed to show him the clothes he shall wear and then the Master of the Wig approaches with a selection. Finally, he gets out of bed and goes to sit by a window in a large armchair. The First Chamberlain removes his nightcap. Another removes his slippers. It goes on and on. People vie for a front-row viewing position. Because Madame Campan is very close friends with one of the chamberlains, she always gets a good spot. She proposes to covertly hand a note to the Dauphin. You see, Vauguyon's eyes are never on Madame Campan. They are usually on me or the Dauphin, and at the rising ceremony they are on the King.

Let us hope it works.

June 22, 1770

It worked! The Dauphin called me to his apartments within one hour of receiving the note. And as if Madame Campan was not brilliant enough, she pressed into my hand just before I left a small lock from one of the jewel caskets. It was broken and did not work properly. She said I should take it to Louis to ask if he could fix it. It was a splendid idea, but in truth I think things would have worked well in any case. I did not show him the lock until the end. Louis Auguste was very upset when he learned that I had written him so many different times. He very awkwardly took my hand in his large, plump, sweaty ones and he actually said, "My dear, I'm so sorry." In that moment I forgot his pimples and his squinty eyes. I then told him about the private rooms that connect to my apartment. He was astounded that no one had told me about them. "I have my forge where I work on my locks and escape the Court. You by all means should have someplace where you can be alone." He is to order their redecoration immediately. When he talked about the forge I remembered the lock that I had with me. He was most pleased that I brought this to him.

In the course of discussing the lock, I brought up Madame Campan and told him how dear Madame Campan is to me, and how I wish she could be one of my Ladies-in-Waiting but that I did not want to offend in any way his aunt Victoire, for whom she reads. Louis then said, "I shall speak to my aunt. I am sure something can be arranged, my dear." Then he leaned forward, for we were completely alone, and I really do think he was just about to kiss me when he suddenly jerked away. "What's that?" he said. His squinty eyes grew even narrower. In a flash he was up from the settee where we sat, and in two strides he had crossed the room and flung open the door. The Duc de la Vauguyon fell into the room. "Scoundrel!" the Dauphin exploded. He turned bright red and seemed to become in an instant like a thick tower of flames. The Duke was scrambling up from the floor. "I beg of you . . . I beg of you . . ."

"Out! Out!" Louis Auguste roared.

So what can I say? I am delighted with the outcome of all things. The Dauphin promises me that he shall send workmen in tomorrow and that the Royal Draper shall come with samples for wall hangings and curtains. I would love to have my walls covered in apple-green silk. And I pray that perhaps Madame Campan can become one of my Ladies-in-Waiting. Everything goes so much better. I cannot wait to write Mama tonight. This will be the first letter in which I do not have to lie.

June 25, 1770

I worry that Victoire might not consent to letting Madame Campan become one of my Ladies-in-Waiting. These daughters of the King are so strange. Sophie, the ugly one, is scared witless by thunder and lightning storms. Whenever there is one, special guards are sent to her apartments and a physician must dose her with tincture of poppies to calm her nerves. Then there is Adelaide, who is very haughty and standoffish. I suppose it is lucky that Madame Campan is not her reader. And finally, Victoire. When Victoire is not being read to she is praying. When she is not praying, she is eating, and when she is not eating, she is playing a set of bagpipes. For the most part, she does all this from her sofa. She does not like to move much. Consequently, she is very fat. But very kind. I love Victoire.

June 26, 1770

The Dauphin and I have been riding twice together and not only that, he has taken me to his forge. Today I sat quietly as he worked on the small lock from the jewel casket. He works with the Royal Locksmith and his instructor Monsieur Gaman. It is a strange place unlike any other at Versailles. It is filled with anvils and heavy, dark iron tools. There are files and hammers, keys, tumblers, and bolts scattered everywhere. I know not the names of half the things I see. Louis Auguste sits on a high stool. His behind hangs over the edges. He wears a leather apron and he squints at the mechanisms of the lock. It is all like a foreign language to me. Still I care not, for I think I myself am becoming a locksmith of the heart, and perhaps through my patience and good cheer I am unlocking the heart of Louis Auguste.

July 2, 1770

Madame Campan will be one of my Ladies-in-Waiting. I am so excited. Victoire says it is fine as long as she is still allowed to read with her every morning and afternoon for one hour. I am of course welcome to come to the readings. I am so grateful that I have asked Victoire if she will favor us one evening with a bagpipe concert. She was delighted. Adelaide and Sophie scowled at me fiercely.

July 5, 1770

Just when I think everything is so good, something bad happens. At least I think so. Perhaps I do not hear correctly. I pray this is the case. We had just left from the King's Rising and gone into the Salon de l'Oeil de Boeuf, which means "eye of the beef." It is a strange name but the King named the salon for the large oval window at one end. As I passed by a close friend of du Barry's, I think I heard a most horrible word uttered: *"L'Austrichienne."* It is a very mean piece of wordplay, for the word *chienne* is female dog in French. So put it with Austrian and it means Austrian dog!

July 7, 1770

I was right about the bad word. I did not make a mistake in my hearing. The Duc de Choiseul, Mama's old friend and the King's chief minister, who first proposed the match between me and the Dauphin, lingered after I had applied rouge this morning. He told me that feeling here in the Court is turning against me. I could not understand why. "Politics," he explained. It is all so complicated. He says there were those from the start who wanted our marriage not to take place. They were hopeful when the Dauphin seemed to ignore me that the marriage would fail. Now that they see we have grown closer in the last two weeks they are upset. Many of these people are friends of du Barry. Du Barry fears that I can influence the King too much. Choiseul himself is a sworn enemy of du Barry. He explains that the reason he wanted the marriage was only for the good of France. He wanted an Austro-French alliance to make sure Mama would never join forces with

Russia or her old enemy Frederick of Prussia. "The Monster!" I exclaimed. "Never!"

Choiseul himself tells me that he is in terrible danger. The King is not pleased with him because he knows his feelings about Madame du Barry. He says, in fact, that both he and I perhaps must make some concessions in order to keep our own positions in Court. He tells me that the King is most displeased that I have not yet spoken to du Barry.

"But she is so coarse, she is so common. Mama would not approve of me speaking to such a woman."

A shadow of a smile crossed Choiseul's face. "For the good of the Empire she would have you speak to her."

His words stun me.

July 11, 1770

Count Mercy, Mama's ambassador, is now here in Court. I see a great deal of him. I have not yet decided whether I should ask him directly this question about du Barry and whether I should speak to her or not. He has not brought it up. So perhaps it is not as important an issue as Choiseul makes it out to be.

July 12, 1770

I cannot help but think about this situation with du Barry. I have written to my mother about it. I told her the King has shown me a thousand kindnesses. He personally is providing new furnishings for my private rooms. But I told Mama that I find his attraction to du Barry pitiful. The King showers her with so many jewels that she can barely find new places on her body to put them. I noticed last evening at cards she had rubies on the heels of her shoes! But I cannot stand her. Does Mama really think I must talk to her? I ask.

But now I worry about that letter. Spies abound here in the Court. It would be easy for someone to intercept it.

Thank heavens I have the refuge of my private rooms. I come here often now with Schnitzy and Madame Campan, if she has the time.

July 18, 1770

The Countess de Grammont is one of my Ladies-in-Waiting, with whom I have become quite friendly. She is a relative of Choiseul's and is most gentle and kind. She was also for a time the governess of the Dauphin's young sisters Clothilde and Elisabeth. Often the little girls come here to see her and we all play. I described to the Countess the mechanical theater of Titi's and she thinks she can find another one for us in Paris. How wonderful that will be.

July 20, 1770

I followed the Royal Hunt today. It was so much fun. Herr Riding Master Francke would have fits. I ride not a horse but a donkey most of the time. They do better on the terrain here. I sometimes follow in a carriage. I always take with me a sack of delights to distribute to the children and older folks in the villages we pass through. And Countess de Noailles is always furious with me. Today I gave a tin of biscuits to a gaggle of dirty little children. They were so happy with them. The Countess just stood there and fumed. I loved it! She is upset if I take my stockings directly from the basket of the undertirewoman, so one can well imagine how she felt about me putting biscuits into the grubby little hands of children — one of whom had just picked his nose! I live for moments like these.

July 23, 1770

My private rooms are nearly complete. They are indeed lovely, with white and gold moldings and apple-green silk on the walls. The sunlight streams through. When I go into these rooms I can be completely myself. And one of the things I do is recall last summer. I think that last summer might have been the happiest of my entire life. I think of that night when Titi and I went wading in the fountains and were joined by Mama. They say the French are joyous, but I think it is a false joy. They do not really know how to have fun. Even if their fountains were clean and well cared for, they would never go wading in the moonlight. Their stupid etiquette would not permit it.

July 24, 1770

I think Madame Etiquette will someday just simply fall over dead from my errors. Today, for example, I saw that as we were receiving in the drawing room the Countess seemed in extreme discomfort. She was twitching and she kept blinking at me continually. Finally, Madame Campan whispered to me, "Your lappets, Your Highness." The two lace streamers of my headdress, which are supposed to be pinned up when receiving noblemen, were still hanging down. One would have thought my drawers were down around my ankles. No, it was just these silly flaps of lace that were hanging down over my ears. I excused myself and had my undertirewoman pin them immediately. She will be in for a scolding from the Countess for having forgotten. But how stupid. In my mind it was worse and much more rude that I ran out on my guests to pin my lappets than the fact that they were down. I despise this etiquette. I think it is childish and silly.

August 1, 1770

Mama writes me a list of instructions once more. In every letter, she writes, "Do try to get your head stocked with good reading." And now she writes to say I should avoid silly novels of romance. This leads me to suspect that Mama is having someone report on my doings. I think it is Count Mercy for he is always here. She also feels that I should pay more attention to the Austrians at Court here, and that I play cards too often with Victoire, Sophie, and Adelaide. She warns me of Adelaide. She tells me I must not ride so much. Now I ask you, dear diary, how does she know all these things? Someone must be writing her. It has to be Mercy. She says nothing about du Barry, however.

August 5, 1770

I noticed tonight at our public dinner how the King's hand shakes. I have heard rumors that he has suffered apoplexy, although no one ever talks about it outright. He is almost sixty.

August 12, 1770

I am very upset. Countess de Grammont, one of my favorite Ladies-in-Waiting, has been removed from Court. Banished! You see, she is a great rival of du Barry and du Barry hates her. One night at a performance in the theater the Countess did not step aside quickly enough to make way for du Barry. Du Barry took this as an insult, and went immediately to the King and complained.

The Countess de Grammont is lovely and beautiful and du Barry knows that she is one of my favorites. She is also a relative of Choiseul, so it is thought that in this way du Barry is influencing the King. But it was indeed wrong of the King to banish one of my Ladies-in-Waiting without first telling me. Louis Auguste is very upset, too, for he knows how much she means to me. Louis Auguste has had the best idea. He feels that we should both talk with Count Mercy about the situation. I think that is wonderful. I love the notion of Louis Auguste, me, and the ambassador to the French Court having a serious meeting together where we can be heard and explain our feelings. It is very grown-up, I think.

August 15, 1770

We had our meeting. I was so proud of the Dauphin. He explained it all so well. We talked in my most private rooms, as we did not want the Dauphin's tutor, Vauguyon, spying on us. Mercy advises me to go directly to the King and gently remind him of the etiquette of dismissing Ladies-in-Waiting in the salons of the Dauphine, for it was indeed an error that he did not at least inform me first.

August 18, 1770

Success! I met with the King today. At first I did not think he would agree. But I used all my charms. He loves it when a woman plays with her hair. I had purposely told my hairdresser to let one long curl fall down upon my collarbone. I began to wind it around my middle finger. I saw the King's eyes fasten on my hand. I began to whimper just a bit. "But, Sir," I implored, "apart from reasons of humanity and justice, think how afflicted I would be if a woman in my service happened to die in your disgrace, the disgrace of banishment." That did it. He agrees to have the Countess de Grammont return immediately.

August 23, 1770

Today is the Dauphin's birthday. He turns sixteen. I have embroidered him a vest. It was a lot of work since he is fat and the vest large. There was a great span of embroidery to be done. But Madame Campan and Countess de Grammont helped me. I also talked to the Royal Locksmith and obtained some tools that he told me the Dauphin would like to have to work on his locks.

Tonight is the birthday supper. I dread it. Three thousand are invited to watch us dine. I do wish just the Dauphin and I and perhaps some of our favorite friends could have just a very small supper in my apartments. It would be so lovely. We could have Victoire and Sophie. I suppose we would have to have Adelaide, and then Madame Campan and Abbé de Vermond and the Countess de Grammont. And, of course, children — Elisabeth and Clothilde and the two little ones who come to play. And yes, we would play all the games that we used to play at Schönbrunn on birthdays. Blind Man's Bluff. Pin the feathers on the chicken. No one really does know how to have fun here at all. It is all etiquette. Our lives are just spectacles. We are like dolls, in a sense, to be observed and played with — often with cruel and deceitful intentions — in an unreal world.

August 27, 1770

I had a terrible dream two nights ago. I could not exactly recall it until today, yet I knew it was terrible. Remember when the *poupée* fell off the bureau at the Hofburg last January and shattered her head? Well, that was what the dream was about. I heard the shatter this time in my dream and got up to gather the pieces together. As I was gathering them, I saw that the face of the *poupée* was not the usual one, for all of Madame Bertin's dolls have the same face, but it was mine. I next heard terrible laughter and I turned around to see who was laughing and it was du Barry. And that is all I remember of the dream. It has made me feel queer for two days now.

August 28, 1770

I have decided to give my own kind of birthday party for the Dauphin. I thought finally, why not have a very private little dinner and have all those people that he and I really like? Then I had an even better idea. Why not make it a lovely picnic like the kind we had at Schönbrunn? I think we should have it in the Groves, for these indeed are the most private parts of the gardens and outdoor spaces of Versailles. In the Groves there are dozens of paths that wind through wooded thickets and natural pools and waterfalls. There are open air glades that are almost like outdoor rooms, perfect for picnics.

August 30, 1770

Louis Auguste loved my party for him. He was completely surprised. I had arranged with his valet and first equerry that they come riding through there on some pretext late in the afternoon. Imagine his surprise when he found all of us there with a table of food and beautiful pastries and wine and champagne. But I think the thing that most delighted him was when I showed him how at Schönbrunn we spread a tapestry right on the ground and ate our food sitting on the cloth. He thought this was the most marvelous thing in the world. He kept calling it an "invention," as if it were some grand instrument like a telescope or a wonderful clock or perhaps a new kind of lock. Then he was dumbstruck with delight when I took off my shoes and stockings and announced that I was going wading in the stream. He had never heard of wading! Can you imagine? I gave him wading lessons. He looked at me with the kind of respect that I might have had for Herr Francke when I watched him ride a stallion and perform one of the more difficult school jumps. I had to keep saying, "It's just wading, Louis. It's just wading."

So, there is one Frenchman whom I shall teach to have fun.

August 31, 1770

The King had a fit of apoplexy today. They say it was the heat and that he overstressed himself hunting. But it was really not that hot.

September 4, 1770

Word of my private birthday party for the Dauphin has spread. Many of course are insanely jealous that they were not invited. But then again they would have been out-raged by sitting on the ground to eat and wading. Everyone except the Countess de Noailles and Adelaide waded. I was forced to invite the Countess. Even Victoire and Sophie waded.

September 6, 1770

This evening there was a grand salon for cards, which means that hundreds of people were playing at tables. Du

Barry made a point of walking directly into my path. I would not speak to her. I simply stared through her as if she were a windowpane.

September 10, 1770

So this Court of impeccable etiquette and manners finds its amusement in making up nasty rhymes about those they hate. The Countess de Noailles tried to protect me from this, but I had heard scraps of it muttered and finally heard it in its entirety, for I made my undertirewoman tell it to me. Here it is. It shows all the handiwork of du Barry and her followers.

Her eyes are blue
her hair ash blonde
her mouth is pink
and her breath does stink
of sauerkraut and liverwurst
The Austrian dog is truly cursed.

Chantal, my undertirewoman, was very upset. Indeed, she was almost crying. Then she said to me, "Your Highness, why don't you make up one yourself about du Barry? I am sure with help you could think of something very nasty, too!"

"I could, but I won't," I replied. "I shall not sink to Madame du Barry's level. Never!" Then Chantal, who is quite tiny, looked at me with her dark eyes shining and she said, "You are a true lady, Your Highness. A true lady!"

I realized that those words from Chantal were as precious as any jewels the King has ever given me. To be liked by one's servants, to be admired by one's servants, is the mark of true nobility. I think Mama would be proud of me today.

September 12, 1770

Poor Countess de Noailles. I know, dear diary, you thought you should never hear such sympathetic words from me about Madame Etiquette. But she burst into my private rooms late this morning and her face was tearstained and ravaged with grief. She had just learned that I made Chantal repeat the loathsome rhyme to me. She drew me into her arms and called me *"Ma pauvre! Ma pauvre!* My poor child! My poor child!" She went on to say they were just words and only a woman like du Barry would either say such things or allow one of her Ladies-in-Waiting or stupid admirers to make up such a thing.

Then she told me how Chantal told her that I refused to make up a terrible verse of my own and she said that indeed I was a true lady and that I had, she now realized, a special etiquette in my bones! Or as she put it, *la caque sent toujours le hareng*, which means "what is bred in the bone will come out in the flesh." This is the first time the Countess has seemed human to me.

September 15, 1770

I worked with the Dauphin today in the forge. He showed me how to clean and oil the tumblers of a certain kind of lock. I did not find the work that interesting. What was more interesting was sitting on a stool next to Louis Auguste and simply talking. He told me that he likes the locks because they are puzzles you can solve. That there is so much in this world that is incomprehensible. Then he said something extraordinary. "Before you came here, my dear, I never thought about the Court and its meaning. Now I loathe it." I was shocked. My eyes filled with tears. Then he quickly said, "No, no, dear Toinette, do not misunderstand me. The Court is a sham, and that is why I have for all these years fiddled with my locks or gone hunting. However, I never really realized this was the reason until you came. You helped me see the Court as it really is. I saw how sweet and direct you are, how pleasant your manners are. I saw your true desire to know a person and that through the knowing, you honor that person. But I never realized this before you came, and now that you are here, and make things so crystal clear for me, I do not like what I see."

I was stunned but grateful for his words. Still, they are unsettling, for one does not like to be the cause of another's unhappiness or discomfort. He continued talking a lot about du Barry and how he hates her but at the same time how he is tired of his aunts and their pinpricking, their *médisance,* as he calls it. He told me that Adelaide is the worst and that even with him she is always talking about his pimples. Then he blurted out, "Toinette, my pimples are awful. I wish I did not have them." I thought for a moment before I spoke and he must have noticed, for I have a habit of biting my lower lip when I think, but I was just not sure how forward I could be.

"What is it?" he begged. Finally, I said it. "Louis, to get rid of your pimples you must drink ass's milk and then at night wash your face in lavender water and apply an ointment of camphor and cloves mixed with oil of hyssops." He was most grateful and immediately called in his apothecary.

September 17, 1770

Louis Auguste and I have been spending more time together each day, either in his forge or in my private rooms. I can tell that this disturbs his tutor greatly because in neither place can he easily eavesdrop on us. He is really such a disgusting man.

September 20, 1770

I notice already an improvement in the Dauphin's complexion. He and I are most pleased. Now if he could just grow thinner. But Louis does love to eat.

September 25, 1770

I am most worried. The Countess de Noailles has been called for a private audience with the King. I am sure this has something to do with my behavior toward du Barry. I hate for the Countess to have to bear the burden of this. Why doesn't the King call me in?

Played cards with the Aunts. Ever since Louis told me how sick he gets of their *médisance*, or pinpricking, I have found it quite tedious as well. They actually never have a kind word to say about anyone. It makes one wonder what they say about oneself once they leave the room.

September 26, 1770

Well, I was right. The King summoned the Countess de Noailles in order to criticize my treatment of du Barry. He says that my behavior cannot fail to have, as he puts it, "ill effects upon the intimacies of family life." Of course, this is all ridiculous because everyone in the Royal Family loathes du Barry except him.

September 27, 1770

It does not take long for words to pass around here. The Aunts all know the content of the Countess's meeting with the King. They invited me immediately to their apartments. They had long lists of advice. They do not want me to give in to the King. Adelaide pulled herself up quite tall for one so stumpy. "It would be an act of disloyalty," she gasped. "You must never talk to du Barry. And be not fooled, Marie Antoinette, she hates you as much as we all hate her. There is another nasty verse circulating about the Court."

The Countess de Noailles almost shrieked. "Princess Adelaide, is this necessary? Please, for the comfort of the child." Then Adelaide practically spat. "Hrumpph. The Dauphine is no child." My head swam. I hardly know what I am anymore. Am I a child? I am a kind of wife but really more of a friend to Louis Auguste. Am I a woman? Am I . . . what am I? I think sometimes I am just an instrument who happens to resemble a human being but serves everyone else's purposes. I do not know what to do or what to be.

September 28, 1770

The smell here at Versailles has been particularly bad recently. I think it is because of the unseasonably hot and humid weather. Today as I was walking with my guards and my Ladies-in-Waiting on our way to the King's Rising Ceremony, we turned a corner just before the Hall of Mirrors and saw a man standing with his back to us. We could hear the stream of his urine! But instead of stopping and reprimanding him, everyone rushed by as if we were not supposed to hear or see anything. That is what I mean about the falseness here at Versailles. It is considered a great offense if I forget to pin up my lappets, yet they don't find it offensive to come across a man making water on the marble floor of a palace.

October 5, 1770

The Countess de Noailles is most upset with me. I have refused to wear the rigid whalebone corset that is in fashion now. It is most uncomfortable and my stomach has been bothering me of late.

October 10, 1770

I have heard a rumor that du Barry is demanding more and grander private apartments and that the King is submitting!

October 11, 1770

Count Mercy visited me today. From his first step toward me in the drawing room I could tell by the deep creases in his brow that he had something unpleasant or difficult to relay to me. He requested to meet with me alone. So I took him to my private rooms with only Madame Campan and the Countess de Noailles present. He handed me a letter from Prince Kaunitz, Mama's most trusted adviser. It had already been opened, for it was written to Count Mercy. It says that to refrain from showing civility toward persons whom the King has adopted as members of his own circle is derogatory and that the choice of the reigning sovereign must be respected. The words might as well have been Mama's, but she let Kaunitz do it for her. I pretended to be very lighthearted. "Yes, yes, of course if that is what is demanded, I shall speak to the hussy." But in my heart of hearts I know I won't. No one can make me.

October 14, 1770

Obviously news of Kaunitz's letter has leaked out. No matter where I go now, be it a performance in the Court theater or cards in the gaming rooms, or a midnight supper in the King's apartments, a path directly toward du Barry is suddenly cleared. Courtiers scatter to the sides, and at the end of the path I see that creature with her thick rosy lips and fat glossy curls. I watch those lips that arrange themselves in a smirk and then I see them begin to tremble as I refuse to look at her but only through her and remain silent.

October 15, 1770

"Just a few civil words, Your Highness. That is all that is required." Mercy says this to me twenty times a day.

"If you dare speak to that wanton, you shall no longer be welcomed here," Adelaide hisses at me, and Victoire, settled on the sofa, toots a blatting sound from the bagpipes as if to punctuate the remark. Aunt Sophie just leers at me out of the sides of her eyes like a nervous rabbit.

"Do whatever you feel like doing, dear Toinette," says the Dauphin.

And the Countess De Noailles just shuts her eyes and shivers.

November 5, 1770

I have been most ill these past three weeks. My stomach
had not been feeling right for some time and then one
night at the card table with Victoire and Sophie and
Adelaide, I became quite ill and nearly fainted. The
apothecary came, as well as the King's physician and surgeon, in addition to my own. They bled me twice. The surgeons here, however, are not nearly as good as those in
Vienna, for they have made a mess of my left foot and ankle from whence they drew the blood. My entire foot is
bruised up past my anklebone. I was so sick that my birthday passed unnoticed. But I am now fifteen.

November 7, 1770

Count Mercy requested to see me while I lay in my
sickbed today. He was accompanied by Abbé de Vermond.
I was shocked when I saw both their faces. Drawn and
thin, both visibly grayer at the temples, I thought they,
too, had been sick.

They got right to the point. Madame du Barry was in a

tantrum. They suspect my illness might have been caused by poisoning! They tell me that the Austrian-French alliance is tottering, that my mother is beside herself. Count Mercy himself has been scolded by the King for his inability to make me speak to du Barry and — they saved this for the last — there is talk of divorce! I should be sent back to Vienna in disgrace.

I see no other course. So I told them that I will no longer refuse to address her, but I will not agree to do so at a fixed hour on a certain day. This seemed to please the Count and the Abbé. They will go to the King directly. Luckily, because of my illness and the terrible bruising to my foot, I have an excuse not to go into public for several days.

November 15, 1770

Snow flurries fly outside my window as I lie in bed. It reminds me of Titi. Oh, how I miss Titi. It seems like yesterday that we were sledding on the brightly painted red sled, whizzing down the slopes of the woods. We ate snow! I said this out loud this morning when the Dauphin was visiting. It just popped out. He turned to me in amazement and I told him about our sledding parties, and how sometimes we would bring a special treacle syrup that we would pour on the snow. The snow and the treacle would mix together and we would eat it. Louis Auguste's little eyes widened in wonder. But mine did, too. "Did you never play, Louis, when you were a child?" I asked. He just shook his head.

I cannot help but think of the fun that Louis Auguste and I could have if we had been born just ordinary people. An ordinary boy and an ordinary girl. I picture us living on a little farm with lots of animals and maybe a meadow that goes to the edge of the woods where we would hunt for wild asparagus.

November 17, 1770

I looked back in my diary tonight to see what I had been doing on this date a year ago. Elizabeth and I were having hot chocolate in her apartments. How long ago and far away that cozy world seems! Look at me now. I have no power and feel as weak as a kitten in every way, and this horrible lady is bending me to her will.

November 26, 1770

I had a relapse of my illness. The King must be worried for he sends two of his own tasters to taste my food in case of poisoning. Now my other foot is bruised from bleeding.

November 27, 1770

A sparkling white blanket of snow lies over the parterres and gardens of Versailles. The fountains are filled with snow and their statues are capped with snowy hats. I was out today for the first time. I insisted. I could not stand to be shut in any longer. I was carried in a sedan chair. Louis Auguste would have come with me in the same chair, for it is built for two, but it was much too heavy for the porters with the added weight of the Dauphin, especially walking through the snow. So you know what that dear boy did? He walked along beside it. Another thing I learned about Louis today on our walk that astounded me is that he has never heard of or made a snowball. So I made the porters put the chair down. I stepped out, although everyone was carrying on as if I were a mad-woman. I bent down, got a handful of snow, and packed it firmly just as Ferdinand and I used to at the Hofburg. I took aim at a statue and hit it square on! The Dauphin was astounded. He couldn't believe his eyes. So I did it again. He positively glowed and then stomped his feet in the snow in an awkward little dance and shouted to the sky, "I have the most wonderful wife in the world! She is the most talented, beautiful creature on God's earth." I laughed so hard my side ached. I kept saying, "Louis, Louis, any four-year-old child can make and throw a snowball." I promised him that when I am feeling stronger we shall have a snowball fight.

$\mathcal{D}ecember\ 3,\ 1770$

The Dauphin came to my apartments this evening extremely upset. He had just heard that the King has banished the Duc de Choiseul. This is very bad news. The Duke was our strongest ally. This means that the du Barry forces have the edge. It is not good. Louis Auguste actually started whimpering. I thought he was going to cry. I said, "Pull yourself together, Louis Auguste. This is ridiculous behavior." But then he said that he is fearful that they might send me away. They might after all make us divorce. I have to admit that for just a moment, I thought, "Oh, now really, would that be so bad?" I could return to the Hofburg, to Schönbrunn in the summer. I could return to an endless childhood. But then I saw poor Louis Auguste's face and I thought, How can I be so selfish? I told him to be calm. We will see this through.

December 4, 1770

I had a very odd dream last night. It was odd yet wonderful. I had been walking alone through the corridors of Versailles. I had gone into the Hall of Mirrors, and in one of the mirrors I saw a reflection of the Gloriette, Mama's beautiful little house at Schönbrunn. I walked up to the mirror and it was as if the glass turned soft and rather foggy and I simply walked through it. I was standing barefoot on the lawn of Schönbrunn. Titi was there and Elizabeth and Ferdinand and little Francis. They were all playing. I think perhaps they were rehearsing for a play or something that was to be given at a ball that evening. I walked up to them and said, "I'm back." But no one seemed to hear me. They just looked through me. "I'm back. I want to play. What part can I have?" Still no one heard me. So I went up to Elizabeth and pulled on her sleeve. This time she turned and looked at me and smiled through her veil. Then something in me made me lift her veil. And Elizabeth's face was beautiful. There was not a pockmark on it. Is that not a strange dream? But why did no one recognize me? I awoke feeling sad but at the same time happy, as if I had actually gone to Schönbrunn for a brief time.

December 8, 1770

Tonight I go for the first time to a performance and then to the gaming rooms to gamble and play cards. I shall decide if I talk to du Barry or not.

December 9, 1770

I did not speak to du Barry. Everyone was expecting me to, and I have decided that I'd rather catch people off guard and do it at my own choosing. I will do it, however.

January 1, 1771

Dear Diary: It is quite late, but yes, I have finally spoken to her. It was at a *petit bal,* or "little dance." I knew I would speak to her tonight, so I purposefully wore no jewels. I wanted to stand in contrast to du Barry, who has jewels dripping from every part of her gown and whose hair is laced with them. Indeed, I wore my simplest gown, but it shows my height and my figure well. There were two occasions when people indeed did clear a path for me to approach du Barry, but I did not take advantage of them either time. I could see that du Barry was furious. However, shortly after the second time, just before the musicians were to begin the piece for the next round of dances, there were several people on the floor milling about. I managed to slip in right in front of du Barry. Everyone seemed startled to see me there. I looked straight at her and said, "There are a lot of people today at Versailles."

How can I describe the expressions that fled across her face within the space of mere seconds? At first it was as if she was so shocked she did not hear the words. Then there was the realization of what had happened after all these months, and that smirk crawled onto her face. A bright hard glitter sprang up in her eyes that matched the diamonds on her throat. But then, suddenly, I saw something turn strange in that glittering light and in an instant I knew what it was. You see, du Barry knew that she had won this single battle, but what did it really mean except for a fleeting glory? Yes, I had been forced to talk to her by the King. But the King is old. He has seizures of apoplexy. He might not live that long and so this victory of du Barry's is cheap — as cheap as she is. And as I stood there, I watched this strange light in her eyes grow dimmer and dimmer.

An eerie hush descended on the room. You see, dear diary, the light drained from the victor's eyes and I, in turn, became a bright and shining woman. I needed no jewels. A silly girl perhaps needs jewels, but I am a girl no longer. I have learned many things in the past year — much more than how to dance and play a hand of cards. Once upon a time, do you remember, Diary, when I was trying not to let Mama fill my head with her thoughts or "invade my nature?" and then I wondered what exactly I meant by my nature? Well, now I know. And I needed no crown as I stood before du Barry, for I was resplendent in my own being. Du Barry knew this. She knew that she was the victor only of the moment and that I, Marie Antoinette, would become the Queen of the century.

Epilogue

Marie Antoinette did indeed become France's most dazzling queen as well as one of the most tragic. Four years after she arrived at the Court of Versailles, King Louis XV died on May 10, 1774. Marie Antoinette was in a room by herself when she heard a commotion and then the cries, "The King is dead! Long live the King!" The new King was her husband, Louis Auguste, King Louis XVI.

The people were joyous at the prospects of this new King and his beautiful and animated young wife. She was, of course, thrilled, for it seemed to her that her destiny had been fulfilled, and she wrote to her mother, the Empress Maria Theresa, "Although God decreed that I should be born in the rank I now occupy, I cannot but marvel at the dispensation of Providence thanks to which

I, the youngest of your children, have been chosen to be Queen over the finest realm in Europe."

Marie Antoinette and Louis XVI did not have children for several years. On the night of December 8, 1778, over one hundred and fifty people were crushed into Marie Antoinette's bedchamber, held back only by the gold railing, to watch as she gave birth to her and Louis Auguste's first child, a girl, Princess Marie Thérèse, named for her mother, the Empress. The spectators in the bedchamber behaved so terribly that what Madame Campan referred to as "the cruel etiquette" of witnessing Royal births was abolished shortly thereafter. The birth of their second child was much more peaceful, and only a handful of people were present to greet the arrival of the new Dauphin, the child everyone thought would be the next King of France.

This, however, was never to be. The tragic tale of Marie Antoinette and Louis Auguste had already begun to unfold long before the births of their four children. Marie Antoinette was a good and loving mother, but she knew nothing of ruling, nor did her husband. She loved parties and extravagances. She was quickly nicknamed Madame Deficit for all the money she squandered. She became addicted to gambling. Meanwhile, the conditions for the people of France, the ordinary citizens, were growing worse and worse. There was widespread hunger and there was a terrible financial crisis, but Marie Antoinette and her husband, shut away in the lavish Court of Versailles, were blind and ignorant to these problems.

Resentment grew. The nobles of the Court wanted nothing to change. They loved their lives of extravagance, high fashion, and endless parties. Marie Antoinette never stopped spending. She loved the fine things that the extraordinary French craftsmen could make, not to mention the fashions of the *modistes*. Fashion and senseless spending reached disastrous proportions and, finally, in 1789, the French people's anger exploded in revolution. The King and Marie Antoinette and their children were put under arrest and taken to a small palace, and eventually to a prison. By this time the Royal couple realized how wrong they had been. They desperately wanted to restore order and peace to France at any cost, but it was too late.

Soon they realized that their lives were indeed in danger. In 1791 they attempted an escape. They were captured, however. In 1792 the Austrians invaded France in an attempt to stop the revolution and restore the couple to their thrones, but they were beaten into retreat.

In August, the leaders of the revolution declared that Marie Antoinette and Louis Auguste had no right to rule. Things began to slide toward their tragic end very quickly. In December, Louis Auguste was tried for crimes against the state and found guilty. He was publicly beheaded on January 21, 1793. The executioners used a new device called the guillotine, invented by a Parisian doctor, Joseph-Ignace Guillotin. The guillotine featured a heavy blade that fell across the victim's neck and cut off the head.

Several months later, on the morning of October 16, a gaunt and worn woman in a ragged black dress was led from her prison cell. She was prisoner number 280, also known as the Widow Capet, a name given to her by the revolutionaries. Also known as Marie Antoinette, also as Antonia, she was loaded into a cart used for common criminals. She was then driven through jeering mobs to a scaffold where the guillotine awaited her. Marie Antoinette was composed. Her last words were to her executioner, whose foot she accidentally stepped on. "Pardon me, Monsieur, I did not mean to do it."

A few minutes later the blade dropped and the people cheered.

The period from September 1793 to July 1794, during which Marie Antoinette was executed along with fifteen thousand other "enemies of the revolution," was known as the Reign of Terror.

One of the most famous of the revolutionaries was a lawyer by the name of Maximillien Robespierre. After the King and Queen's execution, the leaders of the revolution tried to spread their ideas of freedom and equality with the hopes of conquering other parts of Europe.

The commander of the French army was Napoleon Bonaparte, and in 1799 he declared himself the new ruler of France.

Marie Antoinette and Louis Auguste had four children in all. One, Sophie Beatrice, died in infancy. Their oldest son, Louis Joseph, the new Dauphin, was a sickly child and died of tuberculosis four years before his parents were executed. The two remaining children, Marie Thérèse and Louis Charles, shared their mother's prison cell until she was taken away to be executed. Marie Thérèse was handed over to the Austrians upon her mother's death in exchange for French prisoners of war. She eventually married her uncle's son, the Duc d'Angoulême. Louis Charles was held prisoner for two more years after his parents' executions and died in the same prison he had shared with his mother.

Historical Note

The eighteenth-century world into which Marie Antoinette was born was a dramatically changing one. It was a world that was increasingly uncomfortable with kings and queens and the old ways of ruling. Indeed, the atmosphere was laced with the new and exciting notions of liberty, equality, and independence.

In America, the Thirteen Colonies were rebelling against British rule. They saw themselves as an independent nation and not a tax source for Britain. When the American Revolution broke out and the first shot was fired at the Battle of Lexington and Concord, it was said to be "the shot heard round the world," for it seemed to be heard by oppressed people everywhere who were longing for independence. It was most definitely heard by the people of France, who were in fact suffering under the rule of a senseless aristocracy.

Not only was the world ready for these new ideas, but it was easy for such notions to be communicated. Ships were faster, and there were better navigation techniques. Indeed, before the middle of the century there was no precise way for ships to determine their longitude and there were many disasters at sea because ships had no way of predicting landfalls. With the perfection of the chronometer by Englishman John Harrison in 1764, navigators were able to pinpoint their position at sea at any hour of the day or night. Captain James Cook, in the course of three historic voyages, explored and charted more portions of the globe than any person before or since. His discoveries and explorations ranged from Antarctica to the Bering Straits, from Hawaii to Australia and New Zealand. So a new world of ideas and a new world of continents and previously undiscovered seas was opening up.

It was also a time of splendid and very rich art. The art of this period was made to impress, to be grand for the most part, and in many ways as frivolous as the age in which Marie Antoinette and Louis Auguste lived. Thus there was much gilt and decorated furnishings, as well as delicate porcelains. And Versailles set the style. Nothing was left undecorated, be it an inkwell or a chair. Indeed, Marie Antoinette insisted on having likenesses of the heads of her favorite dogs carved on the armrests of her chairs.

But there were great painters as well as craftsmen during this time, such as Antoine Watteau, a Frenchman, and Thomas Gainsborough, an Englishman, both of whom painted beautiful landscapes. And certainly some of the greatest musicians and composers lived during this century, composers such as Wolfgang Amadeus Mozart and Franz Joseph Haydn. The famous German composer George Frideric Handel wrote operas and one of the most famous choral works ever written, *Messiah*. But the music, the furnishings, and the paintings were most certainly for the rich. The poor could not even afford a ticket to a concert or an opera, let alone a beauiful gilt chair.

There is no doubt that Marie Antoinette loved the arts and loved spending money as much on pieces of furniture and decorations for her apartments as she did on her clothes.

The marriage of Marie Antoinette of the Habsburg dynasty and Louis Auguste of the Bourbon dynasty was considered of utmost importance to the stability of Europe, because for much of the 1700s, the various nations in Europe were at war. The three main powers during this time were Austria, France, and Prussia. When one country grew too strong, it threatened the entire balance of Europe. In the northern part of Europe there was another power struggle between Sweden and Russia for control of the countries bordering the Baltic Sea.

The Holy Roman Empire ruled over by Marie Antoinette's mother was really an assemblage of small states in central Europe. Each state had its own prince, sometimes called an elector, to rule, yet the supreme ruler was an emperor or an empress. [This Christian, hence "Holy," Empire began in the time of Charlemagne around A.D. 800 and lasted until 1806.]

From the tenth century the Habsburg dynasty, the family of Marie Antoinette, had been identified with the Holy Roman Empire and Austria. It was in the eleventh century that they became a world power. Their name Habsburg comes from the name of a castle called Habichtsburg, or Hawk's Castle, built in 1020 near Strasbourg, France.

There were two branches of the Habsburg dynasty — one Spanish and one Austrian. By intermarriage within these branches and to other princes and princesses in Europe, the dynasty reached the peak of its power before the end of the sixteenth century.

The situation in France in 1774 was unique in many ways. When Marie Antoinette and Louis Auguste ascended the throne, they did not create the problems that ultimately defeated them; they inherited them and made them decidedly worse. But they cannot be blamed entirely. Both of these individuals had been very poorly educated in comparison with other royalty. Queen Elizabeth I of England, for example, who lived in the sixteenth century, had a rigorous education, even though no one ever expected her to be queen. She also had a sense of inner discipline and knew how to balance her taste for fun and fine clothes with the requirements of governing in a sensible and caring manner. Marie Antoinette had the example of her mother, the Empress Maria Theresa, but although her mother was smart in many ways, and had much to teach, she was late to turn her attention to Antonia and perhaps underestimated what kind of preparation her young daughter really needed to become a ruler in France. Marie Antoinette certainly lacked the political skills and the industriousness of her mother, but she would have been a much better Queen had she been older and better educated when she married.

Louis Auguste was similarly ill prepared. He had seen nothing but a frivolous court his entire life. He, too, was very poorly educated when he came to the throne. Both of them were children when they married and as children had led very confined lives. They had seen practically nothing of a world outside of Court life. They had been taught to appreciate nothing of real value, but they were extremely well versed in terms of material things — clothes, furnishings, paintings, decoration, porcelains, as well as sports and amusements from hunting to gambling.

Their lives were dominated by the ridiculous protocols and rules of etiquette that were deemed necessary for royalty, but served only to remove them from the real concerns of life and governing. It had been this way for two centuries in France. The most important decision either one of them ever had to make each day was what they should wear. In the time of Louis XIV, the great-grandfather of Louis Auguste, there had been even more ritual and etiquette. It was said that Marie Antoinette's *modiste,* or dressmaker, Madame Bertin, was listened to more carefully by her and had more influence over her than the ministers of state. And it was during the reign of Marie Antoinette that hairstyles became even more elaborate, with entire scenes and landscapes built into ladies' towering wigs that were so high that women had to stoop to enter carriages and rooms. Fashion had reached the point of ridiculous, yet people were starving in the streets of France.

It was indeed a strange time in history.

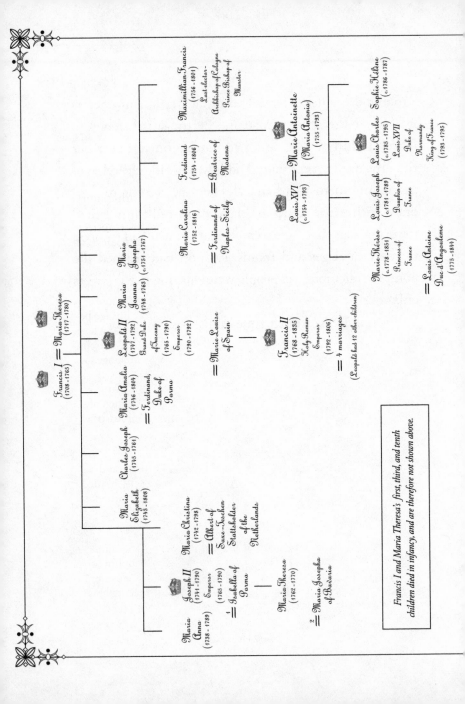

Francis I = Maria Theresa
(1708-1765)   (1717-1780)

Maria Anna
(1738-1789)

Joseph II
Emperor
(1765-1790)
(1741-1790)
¹ = Isabella of Parma
² = Maria Josepha of Bavaria

Maria Theresa
(1762-1770)

Maria Christina
(1742-1798)
= Albert of
Saxe-Teschen
Stadtholder
of the
Netherlands

Maria Elizabeth
(1743-1808)

Charles Joseph
(1745-1761)

Maria Amalia
(1746-1804)
= Ferdinand,
Duke of
Parma

Leopold II
(1747-1792)
Grand Duke
of Tuscany
(1765-1790)
Emperor
(1790-1792)
= Maria Louise
of Spain

Maria Joanna
(1748-1763)

Maria Josepha
(c.1751-1767)

Maria Carolina
(1752-1816)
= Ferdinand of
Naples-Sicily

Ferdinand
(1754-1806)
= Beatrice of
Modena

Maximilian Francis
(1756-1801)
Last elector-
Archbishop of Cologne
Prince-Bishop of
Munster

Francis II
(1768-1835)
Holy Roman
Emperor
(1792-1806)
4 marriages
(Leopold had 12 other children)

Marie Antoinette
(Maria Antonia)
(1755-1793)
= Louis XVI
(c.1754-1793)

Marie Therese
(c.1778-1851)
Princess of
France
= Louis Antoine
Duc d'Angouleme
(1775-1844)

Louis Joseph
(c.1781-1789)
Dauphin of
France

Louis Charles
(c.1785-1795)
Louis XVII
Duke of
Normandy
King of France
(1793-1795)

Sophie Helene
(c.1786-1787)

Francis I and Maria Theresa's first, third, and tenth
children died in infancy, and are therefore not shown above.

The Habsburg-Bourbon Family Tree

The House of Bourbon, one of the greatest royal dynasties in European history, descended from Louis IX, a thirteenth-century King of France.

The great Habsburg dynasty was the imperial house of Austria-Hungary. The marriage of Habsburg princess Maria Theresa to Francis of Lorraine produced sixteen children, thirteen of whom survived to adulthood. The marriage of their youngest daughter, Maria Antonia, to the Bourbon, Louis Auguste, Dauphin of France, provided much hope for a peaceful alliance between two rival royal houses.

The family tree chart shows Marie Antoinette's royal lineage beginning with her parents. Dates of births and deaths are noted where available. The crown symbol indicates those who ruled nations. Double lines represent marriages; single lines indicate parentage.

Empress Maria Theresa: Born on May 13, 1717, in Vienna, Austria. At 19 years old, she married Francis Stephen of Lorraine. She was Archduchess of Austria, and Queen of Austria and Hungary for 40 years beginning in 1749.

Emperor Francis I: In 1736, Francis of Lorraine, Grand Duke of Tuscany, married Habsburg heir, Maria Theresa. He ruled as Holy Roman Emperor Francis I from 1745 until 1765, when he died suddenly of a heart attack.

Marie Antoinette: Born on November 2, 1755, in Vienna, Austria, Maria Antonia Josepha Joanna married the Dauphin of France, Louis Auguste, on May 16, 1769, at Versailles. She became Queen of France at age 18 on May 10, 1774, and was executed by guillotine on October 16, 1793.

Louis Auguste: The third son of the Dauphin Louis and his second wife, Maria Josepha of Saxony. At age 15, he married Archduchess Marie Antoinette. The heir and grandson of King Louis XV, he became King of France as Louis XVI. He was sent to the guillotine on January 21, 1793.

Children of Marie Antoinette and Louis XVI

Marie Thérèse Charlotte de Bourbon: The Madame Royale, Princess of France, born December 19, 1778, at Versailles. She was imprisoned with her mother and her brother, Louis Charles, in 1792. Freed in December 1795, Marie Thérèse later married Louis Antoine, the elder son of Charles, Count d'Artois, who was her father's youngest brother. Marie Thérèse died in 1851 without ever having children.

Louis Joseph: Dauphin of France, born October 12, 1781. Louis Joseph suffered from the disease of the Bourbons, tuberculosis of the bones. He died on June 4, 1789.

Louis Charles: Duke of Normandy, born in March of 1785. He was seven years old when his father was executed and he inherited the kingship as Louis XVII. Imprisoned with his mother and sister, Louis XVII developed tuberculosis of the bones and a severe skin disease. He died in the fortress prison, called the Temple, on June 8, 1795.

Sophie Hélène Béatrice: The last of Louis and Marie Antoinette's children, Sophie was born in the summer of 1786. She died suddenly at 11 months old in the summer of 1787.

Portrait of Maria Antonia at 13 in Vienna, done by French pastellist Joseph Doreux.

Portrait of Queen Marie Antoinette by artist Mme. Elisabeth Louise Vigée-Le Brun.

An eighteenth-century portrait of the portly King Louis XVI.

Marie Antoinette and her children — Marie Thérèse Charlotte, Louis Joseph, and Louis Charles, who later became King Louis XVII — from a 1787 canvas by Mme. Vigée-Le Brun. Daughter Sophie Hélène died that summer before this portrait was completed. It is said that she had been posed inside the cradle but was painted out before the painting was officially displayed.

The steel will of Maria Theresa, Empress of Austria, mother of Marie Antoinette, is unmistakable in this eighteenth-century portrait.

Madame du Barry, mistress of King Louis XV, archrival of Marie Antoinette, as captured by Mme. Vigée-Le Brun.

A woodcut of the grand-scale Versailles Palace with its elaborate gardens. It was the official residence of the French monarchy from 1682 until 1790. Versailles is now a national monument.

A photograph of the Hall of Mirrors in Versailles Palace. The ceremonial wedding of Marie Antoinette and Louis XVI took place in this Great Room.

The French ridiculed the extravagant royals with quirky cartoons such as this one of the Queen and her family, 1792.

A woodcut illustrating the infamous storming of the Bastille, when angry citizens mobbed the prison fortress demanding weapons for their fight in the French Revolution.

Taken from an original painting by Paul Delaroche, this nineteenth-century engraving, done by John Sartain, depicts a plain and somber Marie Antoinette, being led from the court to her execution by guillotine.

About the Author

Kathryn Lasky has always loved history. She says she has always been fascinated by the lives of young people who found themselves in extraordinary historical situations because of their parents. "Princesses and princes had a special fascination for me. They never asked to be born this way and yet so much was expected of them." Marie Antoinette especially intrigued Lasky. "She was so pretty and she was in so many ways so powerless. There was such promise and it all ended in disaster. To me, Marie Antoinette personified all the best and the worst things about being a princess."

Lasky did extensive research into the life of Marie Antoinette. She feels that it is important for readers to know that all of what she wrote is based on actual facts. All of the characters mentioned in the diary are real except for a few. Among those few are the riding master Herr Francke and the servant Hans. It is true that Marie Antoinette's sister Elizabeth had been stricken with smallpox and scarred. However, it is not known if she wore a veil constantly, although many women who had suffered from this disease did. Madame du Barry was most definitely real, and Marie Antoinette refused to acknowledge her in any way. However, in real life Marie Antoinette spoke her first recorded words to Madame du Barry on January 1, 1772. For the purposes of the narrative of this fictional diary, Kathryn Lasky moved up the date one year.

Ms. Lasky first encountered Marie Antoinette in her junior high French class, not in history. It was hearing her French teacher speak of *La Pauvre,* "the poor one," that first kindled her interest. Her teacher, Madame Hendren, explained to Lasky's seventh-grade class that people could be very rich in material things — indeed, like Marie Antoinette, have the most beautiful dresses and jewels and wonderful pets like darling dogs, *les chiens adorables* — but still be very poor in other ways. Madame Hendren explained that in spite of all these possessions, Marie Antoinette had no control and no power; that her life was never her own. That the life of this very pretty and very innocent girl ended in terrible tragedy seemed unimaginable, Lasky says. "Yet it must have been imaginable, for ever since, I have thought about the strange tragedy of Marie Antoinette."

Ms. Lasky says she often thinks about writing a fantasy story of Marie Antoinette, which would tell about a young girl who defies history and refuses her mother's commands to marry the Dauphin of France and instead runs away to America. "She would not be a princess or even a queen," Kathryn Lasky says. "She would be maybe a farmer in New England and join the patriots in the American Revolutionary War."

Acknowledgments

Cover painting by Tim O'Brien

Page 223: Portrait of Maria Antonia, Culver Pictures, Inc., New York, New York.

Page 224: Portrait of Marie Antoinette, North Wind Picture Archives, Alfred, Maine.

Page 225: Portrait of Louis XVI, North Wind Picture Archives, Alfred, Maine.

Page 226: Marie Antoinette and children, Culver Pictures, Inc., New York, New York.

Page 227: Maria Theresa, Empress of Austria, North Wind Picture Archives, Alfred, Maine.

Page 228: Madame du Barry, Art Resource, New York, New York.

Page 229: (top) Versailles Palace, North Wind Picture Archives, Alfred, Maine.

Page 229: (bottom) Hall of Mirrors in Versailles Palace, SuperStock, Jacksonville, Florida.

Page 230: (top) Cartoon of Louis XVI and his family, North Wind Picture Archives, Alfred, Maine.

Page 230: (bottom) Capture of the Bastille, French Revolution, North Wind Picture Archives, Alfred, Maine.

Page 231: Marie Antoinette Condemned by the Revolutionary Tribunal; Library of Congress.

Other books in The Royal Diaries series

ELIZABETH I
Red Rose of the House of Tudor
by Kathryn Lasky

CLEOPATRA VII
Daughter of the Nile
by Kristiana Gregory

ISABEL
Jewel of Castilla
by Carolyn Meyer

While The Royal Diaries are based on real royal figures and actual historical events, some situations and people in this book are fictional, created by the author.

Lasky, Kathryn.
Marie Antoinette / by Kathryn Lasky.
p. cm. — (The royal diaries)
Summary: In 1769, thirteen-year-old Maria Antonia Josepha Johanna, daugh-ter of Empress Maria Theresa, begins a journal chronicling her life at the Austrian court and her preparations for her future role as queen of France.
ISBN 0-439-07666-8
1. Marie Antoinette, Queen, consort of Louis XVI, King of France, 1755–1793 — Childhood and youth — Juvenile fiction. [1. Marie Antoinette, Queen, consort of Louis XVI, King of France, 1755–1793 — Childhood and youth fiction.   2. King, queens, rulers, etc. Fiction. 3. Diaries — Fiction.]
I. Title. II. Series.
PZ7.L3274 Map   2000

[Fic] — dc21   99-16804
                                                   CIP

ISBN 0-439-07666-8

12 11 10 9 8 7 6 5 4 3 2 1   0/0 01 02 03 04

The display type was set in Linoscript.
The text type was set in Augereau.
Book design by Elizabeth B. Parisi
Printed in the U.S.A.   23
First printing, April 2000